"Well, then, let this be a .... tall figure sneered. "And be sure to tell anyone else who gets in the way of my fun that this is what happens when you make *me* mad." He literally tossed Latislav halfway across the room and then turned toward the back door.

Moyra and Driskoll instinctively ducked. They darted down the street, stopping to hide behind the stacked barrels.

Driskoll heard the sound of the man slamming the back door and his thundering footsteps as he made his way up the street.

They saw the man only from the side. But it was more than enough for Driskoll. He would have recognized the tall man's swagger anywhere, even if he hadn't caught a glimpse of his face. There was no doubt about it.

The attacker was Driskoll's dad.

KNIGHTS OF THE SILVER DRAGON

BOOK 1
SECRET OF THE SPIRITKEEPER
MATT FORBECK

BOOK 2
RIDDLE IN STONE
REE SOESBEE

BOOK 3
SIGN OF THE SHAPESHIFTER
DALE DONOVAN AND LINDA JOHNS

BOOK 4
EYE OF FORTUNE
DENISE R. GRAHAM
(December 2004)

SIGN of the SHAPESHIFTER

DALE DONOVAN AND LINDA JOHNS

KNIGHTS OF THE SILVER DRAGON

BOOK 3

COVER & INTERIOR ART
EMILY FIEGENSHUH

MIRROR
STONE

Sign of the Shapeshifter

©2004 Wizards of the Coast, Inc.

Cover art by Emily Fiegenshuh
Cartography by Todd Gamble
First Printing: October 2004
Library of Congress Catalog Card Number: 2004106849

9 8 7 6 5 4 3 2 1

US ISBN: 0-7869-3220-1
UK ISBN: 0-7869-3221-X
620-96532-001-EN

U.S., CANADA,   EUROPEAN HEADQUARTERS
ASIA, PACIFIC, & LATIN AMERICA   Wizards of the Coast, Belgium
Wizards of the Coast, Inc.   T Hofveld 6d
P.O. Box 707   1702 Groot-Bijgaarden
Renton, WA 98057-0707   Belgium
+1-800-324-6496   +322 457 3350

Visit our website at **www.mirrorstonebooks.com**

To Danielle: When you're old enough,
I hope you'll *want* to read this. Love, Dad—D.D.

For T.J.—L.J.

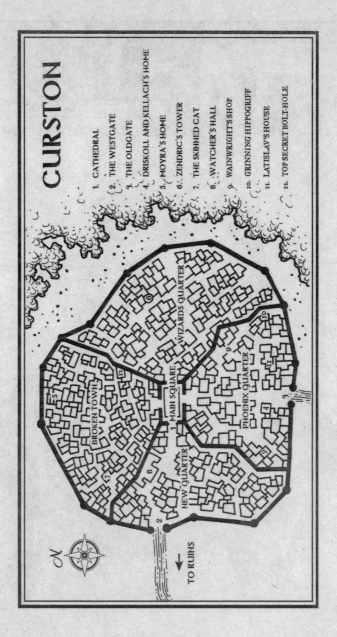

CURSTON

1. CATHEDRAL
2. THE WESTGATE
3. THE OLDGATE
4. DRISKOLL AND KELLACH'S HOME
5. MOYRA'S HOME
6. ZENDRIC'S TOWER
7. THE SKINNED CAT
8. WATCHER'S HALL
9. WAINWRIGHT'S SHOP
10. GRINNING HIPPOGRIFF
11. LATISLAV'S HOUSE
12. TOP SECRET BOLT-HOLE

WIZARDS QUARTER

BROKEN TOWN

MAIN SQUARE

PHOENIX QUARTER

NEW QUARTER

N

TO RUINS

CHAPTER

1

"Do you smell something?" Kellach lifted his nose and inhaled deeply.

Driskoll laughed and held up his hands. "It wasn't me!"

Kellach glared at his younger brother. "What? No, I'm not talking about that." He whirled around, his purple apprentice robes flaring out behind him. Then he sniffed again, wrinkling his nose. "It smells like smoke."

It was a crisp autumn day as the two brothers wandered through Curston's Main Square. Dozens of merchants kept tents and booths there, with almost any kind of food or supply you could imagine.

Driskoll and Kellach were on a mission. This morning their father, Torin, had asked—or rather instructed—them to bring home a long list of food for a gathering of the senior watch commanders the next day. As captain of the watch, Torin sometimes hosted meetings at their home in the Phoenix Quarter. He always liked to have plenty of food on hand to feed the hungry watchers.

The two boys skirted the crowds down a narrow row of food vendors. The bakers' booths overflowed with hot buns, crullers, and flaky pies. At the greengrocers', bushels of apples, pears, carrots, and parsnips leaned up against the tent walls, bringing color to the otherwise gray and brown plaza. A hawker stood in front of a table covered with apples on sticks and shouted, "Maple apples! Maple apples! Get 'em while you can!"

Kellach looked over at the small silver dragon sitting on his shoulder. "Do you smell smoke, Locky?"

Locky was a clockwork dragon. He moved with mechanical precision, but Locky was much more than a machine. As Kellach's familiar, he shared a magical bond with the apprentice wizard. Kellach could understand Locky's chattering language, read his thoughts, and sometimes even see through his eyes.

The dragonet twisted his head away from Kellach and gave a little chirrup.

Kellach looked down at Driskoll with a triumphant grin. "See! Locky smells it too. He thinks it's coming from over there." He pointed toward the Phoenix Quarter.

Driskoll took in a deep breath. "I don't smell anything. I think your nose needs resetting. Here, take a whiff of this." Driskoll grabbed an apple on a stick off the stand. The fruit was smothered in dripping maple sauce.

Driskoll leaned in and touched the apple to his brother's face.

When he pulled his hand away, maple sauce covered the tip of Kellach's nose. A sticky drop fell down onto his neatly pressed apprentice robes.

Driskoll covered his mouth and giggled. "That should fix it!" He licked the sticky sauce off his fingers. "Mmm. Tastes delicious!"

Kellach's eyes narrowed. "Gimme that!" He gave his brother a playful push, grabbed the maple apple, and then started running through the crowded square. Locky lifted off of Kellach's shoulder and took to the air.

"Hey! Come back here!" shouted the fat dwarf behind the stand. "If you don't pay for that, I'm going to call the watch!"

Driskoll frantically dug into his jacket pocket and pulled out a few coins. He didn't know if the coins would be enough to cover the cost of the apple, but he had no time to waste. He threw the change in the general direction of the dwarf and then took off after Kellach.

He may be two years older but he's not much faster, Driskoll thought to himself. Kellach spent much of his time with his nose in a book, studying the magical spells that he would one day use as a wizard. Driskoll loved to read too, but he liked to be outside, exploring the streets of Curston. He knew Main Square inside and out.

Driskoll dashed down the row of food vendors, darting around a crate of chickens. He dodged two sheep, a man pushing a wagon full of turnips, and a pyramid of burlap sacks stuffed with freshly ground flour. But as fast as he ran, he still saw no sign of his older brother.

At this rate, he would never catch up with Kellach, Driskoll thought glumly. He slowed to a walk.

He caught sight of the low wall surrounding the square behind a row of tents, and he had an idea. Squeezing through the narrow gap between two booths, he made his way to the wall and quickly hopped up. As he ran along the edge of the wide ledge that separated the square from the Phoenix Quarter, he had a perfect view of the crowds.

Before long, he spotted a tall figure in purple apprentice robes pushing through the swarm of shoppers. Driskoll smiled and jumped off the wall.

"Hah!" Driskoll grabbed the apprentice from behind and tackled him to the ground. "You cannot escape from my sticky fingers! Give me back that apple!"

"Get off!" a deep voice growled from beneath the robes.

Driskoll laughed. "Nice try, Kellach. But you can't scare me. I'm not going to get off until you give me that apple!" Driskoll scooted forward and sat in the small of the figure's back.

"I said . . . GET . . . OFF!" In one swift moment, the body beneath Driskoll rose. The force was so strong that it catapulted Driskoll into the air.

For a brief moment he was airborne. Then he landed with a thud beneath an herbalist's booth. The plants on the stand's tabletop twisted down to stare at him.

4

Driskoll rubbed his head and sat up. "Kellach?"

The figure stood to its full height, nearly six feet tall. It turned toward Driskoll and pulled back the purple robes from its head, revealing one of the most frightening faces Driskoll had ever seen. Bright red pimples dotted gray skin. A jagged scar cut across the center of the creature's face, from the top of its sloping forehead down to its piggish nose. Bristly hair covered its chin and two sharp teeth, glistening with spit, jutted from its jaw.

It was an adult half-orc.

Driskoll's eyes went wide.

"You," the half-orc sneered. He inched forward. "You tear my new robes."

"I'm so sorry, sir," Driskoll stuttered as he got to his feet. "It was an accident. I thought you were my—"

The half-orc roared.

Driskoll didn't bother to finish. Without another word, he dashed off for the center of Main Square. The half-orc's footsteps thundered behind him.

He darted past a row of wagons and dodged a woman balancing a basket of washing on her head.

He was sure he could feel the half-orc's hot breath on the back of his neck. He ran faster.

When he reached the tall obelisk at the center of the square, he made a sharp right turn and then headed for the rows of booths along the eastern edge of the plaza. If he were quick enough, he just might lose the monster in the crowd.

He darted into the first row he came to.

"Help!" he cried. "Help!"

His head darted back and forth, hoping to see some passersby willing to come to his aid, maybe even some watchers.

But, as luck would have it, he had picked the one row in the whole market that was deserted. The booths sat completely empty. The weathered tents that protected the tables flapped in the breeze.

The sound of footsteps echoed behind him. Driskoll's stomach twisted and his chest felt tight. He wasn't sure how much longer he could keep running. How was he going to get out of this one?

Still running at top speed, he turned the corner at the end of the row. As he leaned around the curve, he dared to peek over his shoulder.

The half-orc was gone.

The footsteps he had heard came from a harmless halfling, walking right behind him.

The little woman looked up at him and smiled as she waddled past. "What's your hurry, boy?" she squawked.

Driskoll watched the woman round the corner, her purple cloak trailing on the ground behind her. Then his face broke into a grin. If he hadn't been so scared, it would almost be funny.

He turned the corner himself and headed back to the fruit stands. When he reached the end of the row, he spotted his brother leaning against one of the booths, chatting with the dwarf behind the counter. With one hand on the booth and the other absentmindedly petting the little dragon on his shoulder, Kellach seemed oblivious to the trouble he'd caused. Driskoll ground his teeth and stalked over, tapping his brother in the back.

Kellach turned around. "Oh! There you are. I was just talking to this nice fellow here. Did you know these delicious maple apples were invented by his great-grandmother? His family has been selling them in the market for the last sixty years!" Kellach smiled broadly. "By the way, he forgives you for your little apple stunt."

Driskoll's jaw dropped. "*My* apple stunt?"

But Kellach was already walking away. "See you next time, Divito," he called to the dwarf.

The dwarf waved.

Driskoll threw up his hands and scurried after his brother.

As the two boys walked down the row, Kellach popped the last bite of his maple apple into his mouth. "So where have you been?" he asked between chews.

Driskoll crossed his arms. "You don't want to know."

Kellach looked at him quizzically. "Have it your way." He began hurrying toward the bakers' stands. "Come on, we've got to get that stuff for Dad."

But before Driskoll could take one step to follow, he felt a heavy hand on his shoulder.

"Hold it right there!" a deep voice bellowed. "You're wanted by the watch!"

2

S-sorry, sir," Driskoll began to say. "It wasn't my fault! Kellach—"

He turned around and looked up to see a tall, athletic boy towering over him.

Driskoll let out a quick little breath. "Oh, it's just you, Trillian."

"*Just* me?" said Trillian. "Is that any way to treat a member of our city's watch? You'll have to do better than that." Trillian gave Driskoll a condescending smile.

Trillian was Kellach's age. He lived across the street from Driskoll and Kellach, and Trillian and Kellach had been friends for as long as Driskoll could remember. But a few months earlier, Trillian had joined up with the watch, and everything had changed. Now he treated the two brothers like little children.

Kellach came storming back down the row, with Locky flapping his wings behind him. He came to a stop right in front of the young recruit. "Hey, Trillian, leave Driskoll alone."

"I am merely doing my duty," Trillian sneered.

"What do you want, then?" Kellach asked.

"Your father wants to make sure you are taking care of his shopping," said Trillian. "He also asked me to inform you that he is expecting you at home for lunch." Trillian pulled a brass pocket watch out of his jacket and clicked it open. He looked back at the boys. "He will be home at approximately seven minutes before noon. He expects you to be there when he arrives."

"Oh, brother." Kellach rolled his eyes. "Look, Trillian, you may work for our father, but that doesn't mean you have any right to tell us what to do."

"Besides, you're not even a real watcher yet. You're just a recruit!" said Driskoll. "And you're not even that much older than us."

"I am a wizard—" added Kellach.

"Apprentice wizard," corrected Trillian.

"—And I'm perfectly capable of watching out for myself and my little brother," Kellach said, ignoring the correction.

"Believe me, no one knows that better than I do," Trillian said. "And I think your father knows that too. Aside from his duty to protect the people of Curston, you two are all he has to live for, now that poor Jourdain is gone. She was such a nurturing mother to you boys, I know." Trillian looked down his nose at Kellach and Driskoll.

Kellach clenched his fists. There was nothing that angered Kellach more than someone making assumptions about their

9

mother, Jourdain. She had disappeared during the Sundering of the Seal—a day, five years ago, when a group of fortune hunters had broken a seal deep in the Dungeons of Doom, releasing hordes of demons. The incident had nearly destroyed Curston. Jourdain had been on the frontlines of battle, helping protect the town. No one had seen her since. But even after so many years, the memory of her was still fresh in both Driskoll's and Kellach's minds.

"Don't you dare talk about my mother!" Kellach stepped forward, his nose a few inches from the young recruit's face.

Locky flapped his wings and poked his long neck forward until it hovered over Trillian's right ear. The little dragon looked over at Kellach for the signal to bite.

Trillian held up his hands and shuffled backward, a sneer still plastered on his face. "Pardon me, boys. I didn't mean to bring up such *painful* memories—"

Suddenly, the cathedral bells began clanging in a rhythmic pattern that could only mean one thing.

"Fire bells!" Driskoll breathed.

Somewhere, a part of Curston was going up in flames.

Driskoll, Kellach, and Trillian all looked up. A huge column of black smoke rose into the sky. It was coming from the Phoenix Quarter.

"I told you I smelled smoke!" Kellach said.

In an instant Trillian's condescending sneer was replaced by a frown. His eyes went wide with panic. "I've got to get back to my post!" He looked at Kellach and Driskoll. "You boys go home. Immediately!"

And without another word, Trillian raced off.

Driskoll gritted his teeth. "Who does he think he is? He's so . . . so . . ."

"Annoying?" Kellach suggested, and began jogging in the same direction as Trillian.

"Wait! Where are you going?" Driskoll asked.

Kellach looked back at his brother as if he were half-crazy. "To the *fire,* of course. Come on!"

Driskoll stood his ground. "But we're supposed to go home. Trillian said Dad's expecting us."

"Dad says that it's the responsibility of every citizen to respond whenever the fire bells ring. The safety of the whole city depends on it. Besides, when's the last time you listened to Trillian?"

Driskoll shrugged. And he took off at a run to keep up with his longer-legged brother.

CHAPTER

3

The boys raced through the Phoenix Quarter, following the scent of the smoke. The closer they came to the fire, the more the streets buzzed with activity. Crowds of people—humans, elves, gnomes, and dwarves—gathered in groups, talking in low voices. One skinny gnome was nearly hysterical. He was already loading his wagon with furniture, clothing, and his six children. When he saw Driskoll's questioning gaze, he shrieked, "I've got to get out of here! The whole city's about to go up in flame!"

When the two brothers reached Pembroke Street, they saw the cloud of black haze rising skyward. Flames licked at the windows of a small wooden storefront. Wagon wheels leaned up against the outside wall of the shop. Directly in front of the shop, a half-built wagon was already ablaze.

"Oh no," Driskoll said. "It's the wainwright's shop! I guess we won't be getting a new wagon this year."

A bucket brigade was already in place. A line of at least thirty people, watchers and citizens alike, snaked from the flaming building to a well at the end of the street. The people in the line passed buckets of water from the well to the two watchers standing directly in front of the shop. As the full buckets reached the watchers, the men flung the water onto the fiery blaze then tossed the bucket away. A boy picked up the empty buckets and ran toward the well. There a blond man pumped furiously, filling buckets that would be handed back down the line.

A watcher stood along the edge of the line, guiding volunteers as they stepped in to help. His face was blackened with soot, with the exception of several tiny rivulets of sweat that rolled down his forehead. When he pulled out a handkerchief and wiped the soot from his eyes, Driskoll recognized his face.

It was Kalmbur, the tall elf who sometimes worked with their father.

"Lads!" Kalmbur cried. "What are you doing here?"

Driskoll was the first to speak. "We heard the fire bells. What happened?"

"It's not clear yet. Gwinton is interviewing McMorley." Kalmbur thrust his thumb behind him in the direction of the stocky watcher and the wainwright. "It was probably just an accident. You know, someone left the stew on the stove for too long . . . " Kalmbur scrubbed at his forehead. He looked down at the blackened cloth and sighed. "First we put it out, then we'll worry about what caused it."

"Is there anything we can do to help you?" Kellach asked.

Something caught the elf's eye, and he turned away to holler at the volunteers. "Straighten out the line! We've got to keep it moving!" Kalmbur glanced back at the boys, with an apologetic frown. "I'm sorry . . . I'm a bit busy here . . . " Kalmbur motioned back toward the end of the line. "Nate back at the pump could use your help."

Driskoll shrugged and began heading for the pump, but Kellach grabbed his arm. "Dris, you help out Nate. I'll be right back."

"What? Where are you going?"

"I have an idea" was all Kellach would say. With Locky still clinging to his robes, he pushed his way into the gathering crowd of onlookers and disappeared.

Driskoll didn't have time to wonder what his brother might be doing. Good thing Locky is with him, he thought to himself. The little dragon will keep him from doing anything too stupid.

Driskoll moved into action, readying empty buckets to be filled by Nate. Driskoll could almost feel the heat of the fire, even as far back as he was. The flames were moving fast.

Driskoll heard a loud crash and looked over to see the roof of the building cave in.

As hard as the people of Curston worked, it seemed like the bucket brigade was not going to save the wainwright's shop.

"Nate, maybe we should start dousing the other buildings,"

called Driskoll to the blond man at the pump. They needed to do something to protect the surrounding shops and to keep the fire from spreading. Nate didn't seem to hear Driskoll, but Kalmbur had the same idea.

"Move the line!" his voice boomed. "Move the line! Dump your buckets on the tanner's shop!"

People immediately moved toward the shop next door that had already begun to smolder.

"The tanner's shop!" Driskoll whispered. The tanner used flammable liquids to tan his hides. If those liquids were exposed to too much heat from the fire, they'd explode, and then there would be no stopping the fire.

Driskoll's stomach tightened. If the Phoenix Quarter went up in flames, that could mean he and Kellach would lose their home too. He began filling the buckets even faster.

Just then Kellach's voice cut through the crowd.

"Make way! Make way! Excuse us. We need to get through."

Sweat poured down Driskoll's forehead. As he wiped it from his eyes, he spotted Kellach pushing through the crowd, dragging an old man behind him.

Dressed in long-flowing sky blue robes, the man hobbled through the crowd. In one hand he carried a gnarled wooden staff. His other hand was busy trying to free Kellach's grip from his robes.

"Unhand me, boy!" the man snapped at Kellach. "I know what's to be done."

The old man broke from Kellach's grip and stumped forward. When he reached the blazing wainwright's shop, he turned and barked at the bucket brigade, "Now stand back, all of you!"

"You heard the man. Stand back!" Kellach repeated.

The old man's eyes rested on Kellach. "Shut your trap, boy. This requires concentration."

Kellach pressed his lips into a thin line, and didn't say another word.

The man closed his eyes, raised his staff in the air with both hands, and began to chant. Driskoll couldn't make out exactly what he was saying above the roar of the flames and the chatter of the crowd. After a few seconds, his staff began to glow.

The sky darkened. An eerie silence descended upon the crowd.

The man's chanting reached its finale just as the staff in his hands flashed. A dark rain cloud appeared out of nowhere over the shop. For a fraction of a second, a huge mass of rain seemed to hover, frozen, directly above the shop.

Then it tumbled down as if it were a huge roaring waterfall.

CHAPTER

4

The water sizzled as it hit the flames. Steam billowed out, replacing the smoke of the fire.

"Driskoll! Hey!" Driskoll was shaken from his thoughts by the soft sound of his name and a light touch on his shoulder.

"Moyra?" Driskoll said as he whipped around and took in the face of his redheaded friend.

He wasn't exactly surprised to see her. The thirteen-year-old thief lived in Broken Town, the poor section of Curston. But Moyra seemed to pop up everywhere.

"What happened to the fire?" she asked eagerly.

"You didn't see it?" Driskoll asked.

Moyra shook her head. "I just got here. Did Kellach put it out with one of his spells?"

"He'd like to think he did, I bet," Driskoll said.

Moyra and Driskoll both laughed.

Driskoll continued, "He found some man who came and

cast a water spell. You should have seen it!"

"What man?" Moyra asked.

Driskoll pointed through the crowd toward the figure in blue robes. The old man was grinning broadly and shaking Kalmbur's hand.

Moyra's gaze followed the direction of Driskoll's finger, and she nodded. "Oh, him."

"You know him?" asked Driskoll. Moyra always seemed to know everybody and everybody's business.

"Yeah," Moyra answered. "That's Latislav. He just arrived in town. He's the new cleric taking over for Lexos at the cathedral."

Driskoll shivered at the sound of their old enemy's name. Lexos had been the magistrate and the cleric of the Cathedral of St. Cuthbert until he tried to kill Kellach's mentor, Zendric. "It's been a long time since Lexos went to prison. What took them so long to find someone to take his place?"

"Curston's not exactly a popular place to preach these days, if you know what I mean." Driskoll nodded and Moyra continued.

"So what do you think caused this? It's not every day a fire gets started in the Phoenix Quarter."

Driskoll rubbed his forehead. "Kalmbur said it was an accident."

At the mention of the watcher's name, Moyra glanced over at the bucket brigade. Kalmbur, determined to douse the last embers, was now herding the group of volunteers back into a line.

Driskoll could see that there was nothing left of the wainwright's shop, but it looked to him that the nearby buildings had been saved.

"Moyra! Driskoll!"

Kellach pushed through the line and hurried toward his brother and their friend.

"Have you seen Locky?" Kellach called. "He must have fallen off my shoulder when I brought Latislav through the crowd."

Driskoll was tempted to tell Kellach he was overreacting. After all, the little dragon could look after himself.

But before he could get a word in, Moyra piped up, "I haven't seen him, but I'll help you look."

Driskoll threw up his hands and joined the search.

The trio slipped past the bucket brigade and pushed through the crowd of onlookers. Driskoll kept his eyes low to the ground, scanning the gutters and walkways for any sign of the silver dragon. As they moved through the throngs of people, he caught snippets of conversations.

"This fire was no accident," said one man whose pipe dangled from his mouth. "If this was an accident, it must be an epidemic."

The group around him murmured their agreement.

Another man added, "It's those tramps from Broken Town. They've been causing all the trouble lately. They're all just a bunch of no-good thieves."

At this last comment, Driskoll could see Moyra stiffen. In Curston, people were quick to blame the residents of Broken Town for everything, from fires to disease to rainstorms to droughts.

"We've got to figure out how this fire started," Moyra whispered to Driskoll and Kellach, "before the watch rounds up everyone in Broken Town."

Driskoll nodded, and without warning, Moyra came to a halt. She confidently walked forward and tapped the shoulder of the man with the pipe in his mouth.

"Excuse me, mister. I'm from Marsden. I'm just here visiting my aunt and uncle. Have there been many fires here? Am I in danger?"

Driskoll tried to keep his eyes down. He couldn't believe Moyra! She was so smooth making up that little lie.

The man puffed on his pipe, seeming to think through his answer. "I spoke too quickly, miss," he said. "There have been two or three fires, but that is not uncommon. What is uncommon is the number of broken windows, burglaries, and general mischief going on here in Curston."

"The captain of the watch can't seem to stop it," added another man.

"Or, more likely, he doesn't care enough to stop it," said the man with the pipe.

Driskoll could stand it no longer. How could they talk about his father like this?

He stepped forward. "Excuse me, sir, I'll have you know that my—"

"Thanks for the information, mister!" Moyra interrupted, and then she pulled Driskoll away from the crowd.

"Why'd you do that?" Driskoll grumbled.

"Because," Moyra said, pointing at the shop directly across the street from the fire, "I just found Locky!"

Moyra scurried across the street and knelt down to pick up the dragonet. "Where have you been, little friend?" Locky was staring intently at something on the wall, right across the street from the fire.

Driskoll followed her, shouting, "Kellach! We just found Locky!"

Kellach hurried over and knelt down next to his mechanical friend.

"What is it, boy? What are so excited about?" Kellach asked the clockwork dragon. Locky responded with clicks and whirrs, never taking his eyes off the wall.

Moyra, Kellach, and Driskoll followed Locky's gaze. There on the wall was some kind of graffiti. Driskoll inched closer. It looked like a sword, tip pointed upward, with a snake wrapped around the blade. The snake's tongue stretched outward, as if checking the air.

Locky flapped his wings and poked his head at the drawing, then looked up at Kellach, expectantly. He chirruped.

"I don't know," Kellach murmured. "Unless . . . ," his voice trailed off. He closed his eyes, and an intense look of concentration came over his face.

"I thought so," he said after a moment, opening his eyes.

"What did you see?" asked Driskoll.

"Locky noticed this drawing because it's magical, or at least was drawn by a magical creature. Through his eyes, it glows, just like the cleric's staff did while he was casting his spell. It's possible that the fire and this sign are connected. I think I need to look into this," Kellach said. "I mean, we should all look into this."

"Kellach, you're making a huge leap," Driskoll said. "Some graffiti on the wall doesn't mean anything. Kalmbur said the fire was an accident."

"I don't know, Driskoll," Moyra said. "I think Kellach could be on to something. You heard it yourself. There have been lots of mysterious happenings around here. Vandalism, theft, arson . . . "

"We don't know for sure that this was arson," interrupted Driskoll. "Accidental fires happen all the time."

"There's no way of knowing unless we look into it," Kellach said firmly. "We should talk to some more townspeople and see if there are any trends. But my hunch is that something is amiss in Curston."

"Something's going to be amiss in our house if we don't get home soon," Driskoll said. "We're supposed to meet Dad for lunch, remember?" Driskoll pointed to the sky. The sun beat down directly overhead. The rest of the morning had passed without any of them noticing.

"You two go home," Moyra said. "I'll keep up my 'Visiting Niece from Marsden' act and see what I can find out for you."

"I think I should stick around and help you out," Kellach said.

"No!" Driskoll said. "We have to get home. Moyra can take care of herself."

"Yes, she can." Moyra put her hands on her hips. "I always take care of myself."

"I didn't say I was going to take care of you," Kellach snapped. "I said I wanted to help you. You may know your way around most of Curston, but I might know a little more about the Phoenix Quarter. Plus, it will be easier for us to get information if we act like cousins. A young girl like you, out on your own . . . ," Kellach started talking fast to get all his thoughts out because Moyra was glaring at him. "Even if you are the craftiest thief around, people are naturally suspicious of a young girl out on her own. Come on, admit it. I might be helpful."

"And that leaves me to return home and tell Dad that you disobeyed his orders," Driskoll said grumpily.

"Okay, I have a better idea." Kellach's face twisted in thought. "Moyra, what if we go home now and meet up with you at about three thirty? Dad will be so busy preparing for his meeting tomorrow that he won't know we're gone."

"I don't know." Moyra looked back and forth at the boys. "Three people on a covert operation like this look fishy," Moyra said. She softened a bit when she saw the disappointed look on Kellach's face. "Shall we put it to a Silver Dragon vote?"

Kellach's hand shot up in the air. Driskoll and Moyra glanced at each other, then raised their own hands in the air.

"Three thirty it is," Moyra said. "I'll come by your window. Now, get going and let me get to work."

Kellach nodded, and Moyra ran off like a shot.

5

D riskoll felt clammy with sweat as he made his way home. Being near the heat of the fire, working the bucket line, and then frantically looking for Locky had been exhausting. Now he was practically running to keep up with his older brother.

The boys raced up the steps to their home. Just as Kellach removed the key from a pocket in his robes, the door yanked open.

"Where have you two been?" shouted Torin. He grabbed each boy's arm and pulled his two sons inside the house, slamming the heavy door behind them. "You were supposed to be home an hour ago! You have absolutely no idea how important it is that I know where you are at all times. Especially now!"

"But Dad . . . " Driskoll tried to explain.

"*Especially now*, I said. If you two were members of the watch, I'd bring charges against you for ignoring my orders. Just what were you thinking?"

Torin looked at the boys' empty hands. "And where are the supplies I asked you to pick up?" Torin looked at the ceiling and gritted his teeth. "It was a simple task. But I can see even a simple task can sometimes escape the two of you. Now why did you deliberately disobey me?"

"We didn't disobey you. At least not on purpose," Driskoll tried to explain, but Torin wasn't slowing down enough to listen.

"Not on purpose? Was it an accident that you didn't purchase the supplies I asked for?"

"We did disobey you, Dad," Kellach spoke up. "We were just about to start shopping when we heard the fire bells. You've always told us that it's the duty of every citizen of Curston to answer the call when the fire bells ring. For the good of the city, you said."

"I know all about the fire at the wainwright's shop," Torin started and then paused. He sighed one of his deep sighs, the kind that seemed like it took him about three minutes to exhale all the air he'd been holding inside. Much of the anger left his face as he spoke again. "I'm not done with you two, but I've got work to deal with now."

Torin motioned toward the study door. Driskoll noticed for the first time that the dark wooden door to the study was closed, a door usually left open unless someone was in there. From the hooks in the entryway hung two large cloaks that didn't look familiar.

"I have guests in the study, and we're likely to be discussing some urgent matters for quite some time," Torin said. "You get some food from the pantry. Since you neglected to buy anything at the market, you'll have to make do with yesterday's bread and sausage."

Torin glanced at the closed study door. "That is all for now. We'll be talking more about this later." He dismissed them forcefully, reminding them both that he was first and foremost the captain.

The boys headed to the kitchen.

"We always go out without Dad's permission and he's never been so upset with us," Kellach said as he tore off a hunk of stale rye bread. "He's clearly overreacting, especially considering we were helping fight a fire. Something else must be bothering him."

"We're lucky he has guests here," Driskoll said, taking a bite of venison sausage. "That seemed to quiet him down."

"Or maybe not!" Kellach snapped his fingers. "Maybe this meeting is the reason why he is agitated. We need to find out what's going on in there." Kellach stuffed another piece of bread in his mouth, and then turned to head up the back stairs.

"If Dad catches us, he'll *really* be mad," said Driskoll.

"Then, we'll just have to not get caught, won't we?" answered Kellach, with a sneaky smile.

The boys headed upstairs, but not to their cluttered room. Instead, they tiptoed to their father's bedroom, which happened to be above the study where Torin was having his meeting.

As they stepped over the threshold to their father's bedroom, Kellach whispered, "Watch out for the board by the door. It's the one that creaks."

"I know. Maybe I should go first. I'm smaller than you, remember? You're the one with the big feet." Driskoll grinned. Their dad had said that Kellach would grow into his feet and end up even taller. But Kellach was still self-conscious about them, and Driskoll enjoyed every chance he got to tease his older brother about them.

"Sssshhhh" was Kellach's only reply.

The boys crouched on the floor near the foot of their father's large feather bed. Slowly, Kellach rolled back the woven rug to expose the wooden planks below. Both boys pressed their ears to the floor.

"This is terribly upsetting, Captain." A woman's voice carried up from the study.

"Upsetting?" a man's voice growled. "It's outrageous! If I didn't know better, I might even suggest that you are deliberately allowing this rampage of theft and vandalism! Merchants and traders are the lifeblood of this city, and we'll not stand for this abuse much longer!"

Driskoll didn't recognize the voices, but their words came clearly up through the floor.

"And what about that 'mysterious' fire, eh?" the man added. "I have it on authority from your own watchers that it was no accident. Nothing seems safe in Curston. I demand to know why the watch seems incapable of protecting this city and its citizens!"

Driskoll looked over at Kellach, his eyes wide. Kellach simply put his finger to his lips and they continued listening.

"Captain," the woman broke in, "please excuse my fellow guildmaster. Mr. Mormo and I share the responsibility for representing our city's merchant guild, and sometimes, he takes his duties a bit too much—" the woman paused, searching for the right word, "—to heart."

Driskoll thought he could hear the man making a "hrmpf" sound behind her.

The woman continued, "What Mr. Mormo means is that we'll have to take matters into our own hands soon, unless you can stop this. We need to know that the watch is looking out for us, as is your duty."

"Now, now, Miss Farley," Torin said strongly but calmly. "I'm well aware of the recent increase in vandalism and other petty crimes—"

"Petty? PETTY?" shouted the man. "You call the fire petty? It could've burned the entire quarter to the ground!"

"The fire was quickly extinguished, as you no doubt know, by the quick-thinking and hard-working efforts of the good folks of our city. I assure you, my friends, the watch is committed to ending this threat and restoring safety to every person who lives within Curston.

"Now, having said that, I do need your help," Torin continued. "I'd like both of you to tell me the facts as you know them. I will take everything you tell me and share it with my senior watch commanders. We will be meeting tomorrow in this very room to discuss the issue."

During the next two hours, the boys learned that there had been eight suspicious acts in the last two weeks. These weren't just simple thefts, but rather they were mostly acts of destruction. An herbalist's shop in the New Quarter had been broken into. Every glass container inside had been shattered, and all the herbs had been trampled. A shop in the Wizards' Quarter selling expensive, fine silks had had every bolt of cloth in the store covered with ink. At the Grinning Hippogriff, someone had destroyed every barrel of ale in the tavern's basement storage room. The list went on and on.

Kellach sat up and leaned his head on his hand. "I had no idea that so much trouble had occurred in the city," he whispered.

"Who do you think is behind it?" asked Driskoll.

"I'm not sure," Kellach said as he rubbed his chin thoughtfully, "but the drawing Locky saw has to be a clue."

"Come on, Kellach. Neither one of the guildmasters mentioned the sign at the site of any of the crimes. It was just a coincidence."

"Not necessarily," Kellach said. "It's possible that no one noticed it."

Driskoll sighed and nodded. When his brother got going on a mystery, there was no stopping him. He was like a dog with a bone.

"There's only one thing to do," Kellach said, dusting his legs off as he got to his feet. "We go to the scene of each of the crimes and check them out with Moyra this afternoon. I wrote down the names of all the shops and taverns." He passed Driskoll a scrap of paper on which he had taken notes.

Driskoll scanned the paper and looked up at his brother. "What about Locky? If we *do* find any other signs at these places—and I'm not saying we will—we'll need his help, won't we? He was the one who spotted the last drawing. Hey!" Driskoll lifted his head and looked around the room. "Speaking of Locky, where did that little dragon get to?"

Creeeeaaaak!

Locky stood on the lone squeaky floorboard, looking curiously at the boys. But instead of walking over to Kellach, Locky walked vertically along the plank.

Creeeak. Squeak. Squeak.

"Shhh! Locky, stop!" Kellach hissed. "Don't move!" Locky froze in place and his eyes whirled, confused.

Driskoll heard footsteps hammering up the stairwell.

"Quick, Kellach! Dad's coming! We've got to hide!" Driskoll glanced frantically around the room. He caught sight of the slim space beneath the bed. He dropped to his stomach and silently rolled underneath the maple bed frame. A cloud of dust flew up around him as he settled into the darkest corner. He had to clamp his nose to keep from sneezing.

"Kellach! Over here!" Driskoll whispered.

"Wait! I've got to get Locky!" Kellach scrambled toward the doorway. "Locky! Come here! Hurry!"

But it was too late.

In the slit of light that filtered underneath the bed, Driskoll could see his father's heavy boots standing in the doorway.

"I thought I might find you in here, Kellach," Torin growled. "How many times do I have to tell you not to eavesdrop on my work?"

"I'm sorry, Dad. I-I was just—"

Torin sighed. "I don't want to hear any more of your excuses, young man. If you're that interested in what's going on down-stairs, you might as well join us. I could use someone to help pass around the mead."

"Sure, Dad." Kellach sighed. "Just let me get Locky."

As Kellach bent down to pick up Locky, he turned and peered underneath the bed. He mouthed to his brother, "Go without me."

And then he stood up and followed Torin out the door.

CHAPTER

6

Driskoll lay in the shadows under his father's bed, torn between jealousy and guilt. Kellach was sure to be punished for this latest infraction, even though Driskoll was just as much to blame. But at the same time, Kellach would get to hear everything that was going on in the meeting. Driskoll sighed. At least maybe Kellach would find out something useful.

Driskoll waited until he heard the footsteps reach the bottom of the stairs and the door to the study open and close. Then he poked his head out from beneath the bed.

Just to be certain, he crouched by the bed and pressed his ear to the floor. Sure enough, he could hear his father apologizing to the merchants for the interruption. The coast was clear.

Being careful to step over the squeaky board, Driskoll scurried to his own bedroom and shut the door. Driskoll gripped the scrap of paper with the names of the crime scenes in his hand, trying to think what to do next. At the same instant, he heard a tap on the window.

He walked over and opened the window, and Moyra tumbled into the room.

"Where have you been? I've been out here for ten minutes! Clinging to a windowsill for ten whole minutes is no picnic, let me tell you." Moyra glanced around the room. "Wait a second, where's Kellach?"

"He's not going to make it," Driskoll said glumly.

"Why? What happened?" Moyra lifted her eyebrows and understanding dawned on her face. "Oh. I take it you didn't get home before your dad."

"Right," said Driskoll. "Unfortunately, he was waiting for us at the front door. He really lit into us, talking about how we disobeyed him and how he needs to know where we are at all times. But he was too distracted to punish us. He was in the middle of a meeting with the merchant guildmasters."

"The merchant guildmasters?" Moyra cocked her head. "Why?"

"Apparently there have been lots of mysterious crimes in shops all around town."

"Pfff! I could have told you that," Moyra said. "In fact, I did tell you that."

"But there's more. " Driskoll filled Moyra in on Kellach's theory about the sign and the idea of searching the crime scenes.

"Kellach thinks we should go check them out." Driskoll showed Moyra the scrap of paper. "These are all the locations."

"Sure, I'm game. But what about Kellach? He's not coming?"

"Oh, right," Driskoll said. "Dad actually caught us listening in on the meeting, or rather he caught Kellach. I managed to hide. Dad's making Kell pass around the mead at the meeting."

"Well, at least he might find out something," Moyra said.

"Yeah, that's what I thought," Driskoll said.

"I hope he'll have better luck than I did." Moyra said. "My 'Marsden' act was a flop." Moyra grinned wryly. "Kellach was right. Curston's townfolk are more than a little suspicious of strangers these days. Let's see that piece of paper again."

Driskoll held out Kellach's notes. Moyra scanned the sheet and tapped the paper. "The Grinning Hippogriff. I know exactly where that is." She looked up. "We might as well go ahead and do some investigating without Kellach, right?"

Moyra unhooked a long stretch of rope from a loop on her belt. She tied one end to Driskoll's bed and dropped the other end out the window.

Moyra swept her hand out the window. "After you!" she said.

Driskoll tugged on the rope skeptically.

"Come on, Driskoll. You've done this before," she said.

Driskoll looked at Moyra, and after silently praying that the knot would hold, he crawled over the windowsill and lowered himself to the ground.

Seconds later, Moyra was climbing down the wall behind him, the rope slung over her shoulder. She hopped down to the ground and immediately started walking east. "Follow me," she said. "I know just the way to go so no one will see us."

Driskoll followed Moyra down a dark alley next to a corner shop that sold rugs. She quickly scaled a brick wall, her fingers almost instinctively going to the random grips she could use to pull herself up. Driskoll made his way up too, carefully watching for the fingerholds and toeholds Moyra used.

"Come on," Moyra said. She was already on top of the building, leaning over the edge and offering a hand up to Driskoll.

He grabbed her hand and hoisted himself up onto the roof.

Driskoll stood up and looked around in all directions. It was remarkable! The buildings' rooftops were close enough together to allow them to move from building to building fairly easily. That, of course, was Moyra's intention and something she knew how to do well. Driskoll had heard about thieves running through the city, jumping from roof to roof. Rooftops were their territory. He could even see some makeshift shelters and sitting areas on different roofs.

The afternoon was clear and crisp. For a city with such rotten luck, Curston almost looked beautiful. Few people ever saw it from this vantage point.

"This is great!" Driskoll said.

"I know," Moyra said, proud that she could share this world—and her expertise—with her friend.

"What do we do now?" Driskoll asked.

"We need to move quickly and quietly up here. Follow my lead. I know you can do it. You know, we're lucky you didn't bring Big Foot Kellach with you."

"Or squeaky-creaky Locky," Driskoll added.

Moyra and Driskoll jumped and climbed across the rooftops for half an hour. Driskoll was beginning to wonder if she was just training him or testing him to see if he could do it. Or maybe she just didn't know where the tavern was after all. Driskoll didn't really care. He'd almost forgotten about their mission because he was having so much fun on the rooftop city.

At last, Moyra motioned to him to come closer to her. "You're pretty good at this, Dris. Ever think about becoming a thief?" she asked, half joking.

Driskoll grinned. "That would really give my dad something to complain about, wouldn't it?"

"Okay, you can be my apprentice today." Moyra laughed. "Come on, Apprentice. This way, to the Grinning Hippogriff."

Moyra leaped over a slim gap between two rooftops and led Driskoll high above a narrow winding road. They hadn't crossed more than two buildings when Moyra stopped and grabbed Driskoll's arm, motioning the boy to be quiet.

She stiffened and seemed to be holding her breath.

"Did you hear that?" she whispered. "Listen!"

A stifled cry floated up to the roof. It sounded close. They both held their breath.

Crash! The sound of breaking glass came from across the street. They hurried to the edge of the roof to have a better view. They lay on their stomachs and inched to the very edge. They heard glass break again. It sounded like a bar fight of some sort.

Driskoll leaned over the rooftop and peered out. The noises sounded as if they were coming from a small one-story home across the street. It was painted gray and had a white doorway with what looked like a small archery target hanging on the door.

"That's not the Grinning Hippogriff," Driskoll whispered.

"I know." Moyra pulled Driskoll back a bit from the roof's edge. "That's where Latislav lives. Look . . . " Moyra pointed at the tiny wooden sign mounted on the door. "That's the symbol of St. Cuthbert."

Driskoll nodded impatiently. Of course he knew the symbol of St. Cuthbert.

"It sounds like he's in trouble. We should do something."

This time Driskoll took the lead. He moved to the roof's edge, grasped it with both hands, swung down until he was hanging just by his fingertips, and then dropped to the ground. It was a long drop, and he managed to land on the dirt, just inches away from two stacked barrels.

Moyra landed right after him. "Nice job!" she said.

Driskoll couldn't help but smile. He looked quickly around them. It didn't seem like anyone had seen them. They crept around the side of the cleric's house until they found the back door. At the top of the door was a small window, which now lay in shatters around them. Moyra and Driskoll rose up to peer inside.

They were looking directly into Latislav's kitchen. The cleric was there. But so was someone else.

Latislav was backed up against the far wall, clinging to his wooden staff. He held it up, trying to avert the blows of his tall attacker.

"Spoil my fun, will you?" the attacker snarled at the cleric. "I go to all the trouble to start that lovely fire, and you have to show up and put . . . it . . . out." Each of his final words was punctuated by a kick at the old man.

Latislav sagged to the floor, but his attacker lifted him up—with one arm. He held the battered and bleeding cleric like a rag doll. Driskoll wished the man would turn so they could get a look at his face.

"Well, then, let this be a lesson," the tall figure sneered. "And be sure to tell anyone else who gets in the way of my fun that this is what happens when you make *me* mad." He literally tossed Latislav halfway across the room and then turned toward the back door.

Moyra and Driskoll instinctively ducked. They darted down the street, stopping to hide behind the stacked barrels.

Driskoll heard the sound of the man slamming the back door and his thundering footsteps as he made his way up the street.

They saw the man only from the side. But it was more than

enough for Driskoll. He would have recognized the tall man's swagger anywhere, even if he hadn't caught a glimpse of his face. There was no doubt about it.

The attacker was Driskoll's dad.

CHAPTER

7

Driskoll looked at Moyra. His face felt hot and he swallowed hard at the lump in his throat.

"Was that my . . . " Driskoll gulped. "My dad?"

Moyra wouldn't look him in the eye. "We have to help Lasitlav," she said quietly. She stood up and headed for the cleric's back door. Driskoll, still stunned, followed.

The cleric was alive, but unconscious on the kitchen floor. Moyra found a rag and a wooden cup. She ran back outside, dipped the cloth in the water trough and filled the cup with cool water. She went back inside and wiped some blood from the man's face, then placed the cool, wet cloth on his forehead. Bruises were already forming on his face.

Driskoll just stood there, in the corner of the kitchen.

"Is he . . . is he going to be all right?" Driskoll asked with a shaky voice.

"I hope so," Moyra answered. "We need to stay with him

until we know if we need to get extra help."

Latislav moaned and his eyes fluttered open. He looked up at Moyra, and then frantically glanced around the room. He was clearly terrified.

"It's okay now," Moyra whispered to Latislav. "Tor—I mean, the man—he's gone. Here, sip this water." She lifted the cup to his swollen lips.

Latislav drank gratefully, and then he leaned back against the wall.

"Thank you, my child, thank you. Who are you two?" He looked over at Driskoll then back at Moyra again.

"We were just passing and heard the noise. We saw the broken window and we came inside." Moyra was talking quickly. "How do you feel? Do you think you'll be all right? Or should we go get some help?"

"Child, I'll be fine. I've had worse thrashings in my day, but not for many a year now. St. Cuthbert will help me recover. But you didn't answer my question. Who are you and what are you doing here? And you?" He turned toward Driskoll. "Who are you, lad?"

"Ummm, we have to go." Moyra quickly set the cup on the floor next to the cleric and stood up. "It's getting late, and we need to get home before curfew." Moyra crossed the room, grabbing Driskoll's arm as she passed and pulling him toward the door.

Latislav pushed against the wall behind him to stand. He

reached out, his arm sweeping the air in front of him, as if he could grab Moyra and keep her from slipping out the door. "Wait! What are your names? You've been very kind to an old man, and I'd like to thank you and your family—"

"I hope you feel better soon," said Moyra. With a weak wave, she and Driskoll ran out the door.

The two kids hurried down the block. Driskoll's mind was racing. He had a million questions. Was Latislav's attacker really his dad? Why would Torin want to attack a harmless cleric? Driskoll knew what he had seen and, yet, he just couldn't bring himself to believe it.

"Moyra, I know what you think you saw, but there's no way that was my dad," Driskoll said. "You believe that, right?"

In answer, Moyra turned and gripped the wall of the building behind them. She rested her boot on a large stone outcropping about a foot off the ground. But she did not turn around.

"Look. I can't talk now, Dris. It's nearly curfew, and my mom's waiting for me. We-we can talk about it tomorrow." She scaled the wall, hopped up on the low rooftop, and then she was gone.

Driskoll was tempted to climb up the wall and follow her. But somehow it didn't seem like fun anymore.

He ran back to the Phoenix Quarter with the sun setting behind him, casting a yellowish glow over the city. Reaching his home, he slowly opened the door and slipped inside, praying that the old door wouldn't creak.

The cloaks that had hung in the hallway were gone, and the study was dark. It looked like everyone was gone.

He tiptoed up the stairs and entered his and Kellach's shared bedroom, kicking off his boots as he came through the door.

Kellach was sitting up in his bed, his nose stuck in his spellbook. The book had once been their mother's, and Driskoll often caught his brother looking at it even when he wasn't studying spells.

Kellach lifted his head from the slim volume. "How'd it go? Did you find the sign?"

"We didn't exactly make it that far." As Driskoll changed into his nightclothes, he told him everything. Kellach listened and nodded grimly.

"It doesn't make any sense," Driskoll finished, crawling into bed. "Dad was here all evening, right?"

"Yes, but . . . " Kellach leaned back and put his arm under his head, staring up at the ceiling. "After you left, the guildmasters shouted at Dad for about half an hour more. They drank the mead, and then they left. Dad was really angry, at them and at me. He yelled at me for spying, and told me how I had embarrassed him in front of the guildmasters. But that wasn't the worst part."

"What do you mean?"

Kellach turned and looked Driskoll in the eye. "He took Locky."

"What? No!"

Kellach nodded. "He locked him in his bedroom closet and said that I could have him back after I had learned some respect. Poor Locky. It wasn't his fault."

Driskoll almost thought he could see tears in his older brother's eyes.

Kellach cleared his throat and continued. "Then Dad said he was leaving early for work, for the evening patrol. He's been gone ever since. That was about a half an hour ago."

Driskoll's face brightened. "There's no way Dad could have gotten over to Latislav's and attacked him in the last half an hour!"

"Well, it is *possible*," Kellach said. "But highly unlikely. There's no way of knowing for sure unless we have some proof." Kellach rubbed his chin thoughtfully.

Driskoll's face settled back into a frown, and he nodded glumly. "What kind of proof?"

"I'm not sure yet, but don't worry. I'll think of something." Kellach blew out the candle by their beds.

But neither boy slept well that night.

CHAPTER

8

The next morning, dark storm clouds hovered over the city, as if the sky were in a foul mood. Rain hammered down on the rooftop, waking Driskoll from a restless sleep.

Torin was too consumed with the morning meeting of the watch commanders to notice the dark circles under his son's eyes. Driskoll carefully studied his father's face, trying to get an answer to what he'd seen last night. An answer to *something*. To anything. But Torin's stoic face showed no emotion.

As always, the duties for preparing food fell to Driskoll and Kellach. Feeling bad about what had happened to Kellach yesterday, Driskoll volunteered to run to the market for fresh rolls, while Kellach agreed to stay home and make the tea. Once he returned, Driskoll methodically placed the honey, the apple butter, and the fresh rolls on the table in the study. Kellach stacked the cups.

46

Soon there was a knock on the door.

"Dad, the watch commanders are here!" Driskoll opened the door, and then drew back in surprise.

There weren't any watchers on the doorstep.

Instead, an angry mob gathered in front of the house, oblivious to the pouring rain.

As soon as the door opened, they began to shout, "Justice for Torin! Justice for Torin!"

Driskoll quickly shut the door and hurried to the window. Several people in the crowd saw his face in the window and pointed their fingers at him.

"Daaaaaaad," Driskoll called out. "You'd better come look at this."

Torin made his way to the window just as the chants began again.

"Torin! Torin! Torin!" The crowd was calling for him to come out.

"Now what?" Torin said to no one in particular. "Kellach, go out and see what they want."

"But, Dad," Kellach broke in, "they're calling for you to go out and talk to them."

"Fine, fine, fine," Torin said with a heavy sigh. He cleared his throat, patted down his clothes to brush off any crumbs, and stepped out onto the front steps.

"Good morning, citizens," Torin called out. "What brings you to my door this morning? How may I help you?"

In answer, at least ten people began to talk, shout, wave, and shake fists at Torin.

"Please, please." Torin lifted his hand to calm the crowd. "One at a time. I can't help unless I know what the problem is."

"You're the problem, you brutal man," came an aged but firm voice.

Latislav hobbled to the front of the crowd. He looked much better than he had just yesterday afternoon, but it was still clear that the man had gotten a savage beating.

Most of his face was swollen. His left eye was puffed up to the point he could barely open it, and in the gray light of morning, nasty purple bruises stood out on his jaw, his neck, and around his right eye.

"You attacked me in my own home yesterday evening, you, you blackguard!" Latislav shouted while leaning on his staff for support. Several people in the crowd echoed his anger.

"I did what, sir?" Torin screwed up his face in a look of puzzlement. "It is clear you've been injured. May I offer you the services of the watch's healers?"

"I want nothing from you but justice," Latislav answered. "You admitted that you had started the fire in the wainwright's shop. You said I spoiled your fun by putting it out."

"I've been informed of your heroic action yesterday, sir, by one of my men last night. On behalf of the city, I thank you. You may have prevented a catastrophe."

"Aye, and this is the thanks you gave me," replied Latislav, pointing to his bruised face.

"Tell me, when did this attack take place?" asked Torin.

"About half an hour before curfew," replied Latislav. The crowd had quieted now, turning from angry to attentive. They wanted to hear the discussion between the two men.

By this time, a few of the watch commanders had arrived. They were standing outside, clearly puzzled by the crowd, and watching their captain intently.

Torin laughed. "Well, then, it's settled. At that time yesterday, I was here meeting with guildmasters Mormo and Farley on matters of mutual import."

Kellach and Driskoll exchanged worried glances. They knew their father wasn't exactly telling the whole truth, but they certainly didn't want to say so given this angry crowd.

"Earlier that morning," Torin continued, "I was at Watchers' Hall. I doubt I could have slipped past an office full of watchers to start a fire in the Phoenix Quarter. Are there any witnesses here to say they saw me anywhere near the fire or the scene of your attack?"

Latislav raised his bruised face and looked up at the window where Driskoll stood. Driskoll felt like throwing up. He could feel the old man's eyes on him, as if they were burning holes, straight through his heart. Kellach put a comforting hand on his brother's back.

"Now, Latislav," Torin went on, "it's clear a dire crime has been committed against you. I do not doubt your wounds, nor your account of events. However, I do suggest that an imposter, someone who intended to frame me for the fire, may have attacked you. Is that not at least a possibility? I ask you, could you not have been deceived in some manner?"

"I'd swear on St. Cuthbert's cudgel that it was you, but it is possible that some cunning disguise could have been used by another to look like you. But if so, it was the most uncanny disguise I've ever seen."

The crowd was silent. Many of the folks started looking at each other, unsure now of what to believe about the events of the day before. Then a tall elf stepped out from behind the cleric.

"Latislav's not the only one who has a bone to pick with you, Captain! I have an eyewitness that puts *you* not ten feet from my shop on the very night it was vandalized."

Torin chuckled. "Now, now, Shankus. You know I patrol that street almost every evening! I dare say that's just a coincidence at best."

"Aye!" a man with a ratted beard shouted. "I heard someone say you were at the Grinning Hippogriff the day those barrels of ale were destroyed! You call *that* a coincidence, Captain?"

As the crowd began to shout again, a door across the street opened. Trillian came out, hurriedly pulling on his watcher jacket. He pushed through the crowd and rushed up the steps of Kellach and Driskoll's home.

"Sir! Is everything all right?"

"Ah! Trillian, you're right on time." Torin gestured to Latislav, still glaring up at him from the street. "Would you kindly escort our heroic cleric to Watchers' Hall to take his full statement and see to his wounds?"

Torin turned back to address the crowd. "Any of the rest of you who may have information about unsolved crimes, please make your way to Watchers' Hall. My watchers there will take your statements." Torin took in a deep breath. "There is no doubt that Curston is suffering from a crime spree. But I assure you I am not to blame. The watch is doing all we can to find the real criminals, with your kind assistance. Now please, go about your business so we of the watch can go about ours. Thank you."

As Trillian led Latislav and the other accusers off toward the New Quarter, the crowd began to disperse. Torin stepped off the stoop to speak briefly to the watch commanders. Then together, they headed off toward Watchers' Hall.

Now that the crowd had thinned out, Driskoll spotted Moyra across the street. She saw him, too, and waved. She headed to the back of the house, and the boys met her there.

Outside, the pounding rain had slowed to a drizzle. Moyra's perky red waves lay mashed against her head. The girl obviously hadn't slept much, if at all. Her eyes were bloodshot, and her fair skin was even paler than usual.

"I don't know what to say." Moyra looked at Kellach. "Dris told you, right? He told you what we saw?"

"Yes, Dris told me what you thought you saw," Kellach said.

"Thought we saw? Thought? I know what I saw. I *saw* your father attack an innocent man!" Moyra practically shouted.

"But didn't you hear what Dad just said outside?" Driskoll asked. "He was home when the attack occurred."

"Of course Torin would say he was home," Moyra said. "When confronted with a crime, deny it. Every common criminal knows that."

"*You* would know." Driskoll crossed his arms.

"Dris, that's enough," Kellach said. But Driskoll couldn't stop himself now. He was mad, not apologetic.

"Look," Driskoll continued. "Did you ever consider that the attacker could have been an imposter? Maybe the attacker even knew that you and I'd be there, and knew that the perfect cover would be to pretend to be Dad." Driskoll felt his face grow hot and he clenched his fists. "You're so ready to believe my dad is a criminal. And I know why: it's because you hate my father! You want to destroy him because you're angry that he keeps catching your dad at his stupid schemes. Your dad is just a no-good thief—and so are you!"

Moyra's eyes narrowed. "For the record, my father's schemes are not stupid. And I'm one of the best thieves in all of Curston. And, more importantly," her voice rose even louder now, "I do not hate your father."

"Liar!" Driskoll snapped.

Moyra turned to Kellach. "Please say you believe me, Kell.

Driskoll just doesn't want to admit it. But I know what we saw. If you're really my friend, you will trust me on this."

Kellach was deep in thought, but he managed to mutter, "Maybe you just didn't see the attacker *clearly* . . . "

Moyra's face flushed bright red. "If that's how you feel, I hope I never have to see either of you ever again!"

And with that, Moyra stormed off down the street.

CHAPTER

9

Neither boy said anything for several minutes.

"We're better off without her," Driskoll finally announced. He sat down on the back steps.

Kellach sighed and sat down next to him.

"Listen," Driskoll began. "I know I got a little carried away there. But the more I think about it, the more I'm sure Dad wasn't involved. What do you think? What were you going to say before Moyra left?"

"I was just going to say that we have to think about this logically. I know what you and Moyra thought you saw. I also know our father. True, there's a slim chance that he could have been at Latislav's last night. But attacking a cleric in his own home, for no reason? It's just not like him. There must be some other explanation."

Driskoll nodded. "Right. Even if Dad had the means and opportunity, what's his motive? Why would he want to set a fire that would destroy the whole city? Or vandalize shops and taverns? It only makes the watch look bad! And why would he hurt an old man like Latislav? Dad might be strict, but he's not a brute." Driskoll propped his head up in his hands.

Then his eyes went wide. "I've got it! Maybe it's some kind of mind control! Remember what happened last time . . . at the Promise Festival?"

Kellach shook his head. "No, I don't think that's it exactly. But I do think someone is trying to make Dad look bad." Kellach rubbed his chin, deep in thought.

"Whoever it is, that's one great disguise they're using. I mean, you should have seen it, Kell. The guy who attacked Latislav looked *exactly* like Dad. *Exactly.*" Driskoll took in a quick breath. "Hey, remember how you said you thought that symbol was made by a magical creature?"

"Yeah . . ."

"Well, there is one magical creature I can think of that can impersonate almost anything."

"What's that?"

"The Trickster! Don't you remember? Mom taught us a rhyme about the Trickster when we were little."

Driskoll began to recite in a singsong voice.

Watch out, watch out
You'll never know
Just what face the Trickster shows

From dwarf to elf
To babes in arms
He'll change his shape
To do you harm

Watch out, watch out
You'll never know
Just what face the Trickster shows

"Oh, give me a break." Kellach scoffed. "The Trickster isn't real! That's just a baby rhyme! And a stupid one at that."

Driskoll looked at the ground. "It was just an idea."

"But," Kellach said, rubbing his hands together. "I do think the key to this mystery lies in that symbol we saw outside the wainwright's shop. Whoever is committing these crimes is leaving this sign as a clue."

"But what does the sign mean?" Driskoll asked.

"I'm not sure yet, but I'm going to find out. Come on, let's get to work. I've got to get to Zendric's tower in less than forty minutes for my lesson."

"What about Locky? Do you think we can find the signs without him?"

"I'm practically a wizard now." Kellach stood up, straightening his robes and lifting his chin as if posing for a picture. "And I'm perfectly capable of spotting a magical sign. Let's start with the latest crime—Latislav's home."

Driskoll grinned, happy to be on the trail to proving their father's innocence. He stood up and began walking down the street. "Follow me!" he said.

The two boys wound through the streets of the Phoenix Quarter. It was hard to remember exactly where the cleric's home was, given that yesterday, Driskoll had made his way there via the rooftops. But after a few wrong turns, he finally came to a stop.

"That's it," Driskoll said, pointing toward a small wooden structure. "That's where Latislav lives . . . where we found him last night."

"All right," said Kellach. "Dris, you look on that side of the street, but be nonchalant about it. Don't look like you're looking for something. Whoever did this could still be around here somewhere."

If he had had had more sleep the night before, he'd have had a smart comeback to Kellach's instructions. Driskoll was a master of nonchalance. It was the storyteller in him, wanting to observe everything and learn everyone's tales. He was much like Moyra in that he'd learned how to blend into a crowd and go unnoticed.

Driskoll searched high and low on the surrounding buildings and houses, around the corner and down the street. Nothing. No drawings. Certainly nothing magical or with a mysterious symbol.

He was about to give up when he heard Kellach whistle.

Driskoll spotted his brother crouching near the water trough almost directly across from where Latislav lived.

Driskoll crossed the streed and squatted next to his brother.

Kellach pointed to the far side of the trough, the side that faced away from Latislav's house. There was the strange sword symbol. It was hard to notice at first since it was so close to the wall of the house it stood next to. But Kellach's sharp eyes had spotted it. It looked exactly like the symbol near the wainwright's shop, down to the size and shape of the sword. Kellach had been right.

"The same kind of charcoal," Kellach said, "the same style. But I can't decipher if it was drawn by a magical creature or if the symbol itself is magical."

He frowned and pulled out a piece of parchment from his spellbook. Using a pencil he had found in his pocket, he began copying the symbol.

"Maybe Zendric will know something about the sign," Driskoll suggested. "Can you ask him at your lesson today?"

"That's exactly what I was thinking." Kellach put the finishing touches on his drawing, then waved the paper underneath Driskoll's nose. "Does that look about right?"

Driskoll scanned the crude sketch. The wide squiggles bore nothing but a vague resemblance to the symbol on the trough. Kellach was no artist, that was for sure. Driskoll lifted his shoulders and opened his mouth to speak. But Kellach already had a ready answer.

"It's excellent, isn't it?" Kellach snatched back the paper and looked it over himself, with a satisfied grin on his face. "If it weren't for my talent for spellcasting, I would have become a painter's apprentice." He stuffed the paper into his spellbook, and stood up. "Okay, we have a potential pattern here. Let's take a look at the other sites. If we move quickly, we can check out a few other places before I have to go to my lesson."

Forty minutes and four sore feet later, the boys had a few more answers—and many unanswered questions. They'd visited every crime scene they'd heard of, including the Grinning Hippogriff. Each one did have the mysterious symbol somewhere nearby.

It was time for Kellach to report to Zendric's tower, and despite Kellach's mild protests, Driskoll insisted on walking him there. He wanted to hear exactly what Zendric would have to say about the signs they'd found and the recent crime spree.

As the two boys wound through the city toward Zendric's tower, Driskoll couldn't shake the feeling that they were being followed. He kept glancing over his shoulder, but no one was there.

Outside one shop filled with nothing but magical stones, Driskoll stopped and looked behind him. A dark-haired teenage boy in a purple shirt stood across the street casually looking in a window. When he caught Driskoll's looking at him, the boy took a turn to the right and wandered off down a side street. Driskoll shook his head to clear it. He must be imagining things.

When they reached Zendric's street, Kellach began to walk faster. He pushed through the gate and entered the yard. It was all Driskoll could do to keep up with him.

But when Kellach came to the front of the tower, he paused.

"What are you waiting for?" Driskoll asked when he caught up with him. "You better get in there now, or Zendric will have a fit. Remember last week when you were thirty seconds late? Zendric yelled at you for about fifteen minutes."

Kellach didn't answer. He just kept staring at the doorway.

Driskoll followed his brother's gaze down to the doorjamb, and suddenly he realized why Kellach had stopped.

The door was open.

CHAPTER

10

The boys exchanged nervous glances.

"You don't think . . . " Driskoll began. But he couldn't bring himself to say it aloud. The last time they had found the door to Zendric's tower open, it had nearly spelled the end of Zendric and all of Curston. Driskoll's stomach tightened.

"I don't know what's going on, but I think we should be careful." Kellach tiptoed over the threshold. His eyes darted around the room nervously.

"Hellooo! Zendric?" Driskoll called halfheartedly. His heart pounded in his ears. He followed his brother through the door, scanning the room as he went. The first floor of Zendric's tower served as a classroom for Zendric's lessons with Kellach and other students. Books were stacked neatly across the mantel of the fieldstone fireplace on one side of the room. A fat armchair sat in front of the hearth. A row of writing desks, separated by green velvet curtains, lined the back wall of the chamber.

Instructional tapestries, detailing famous spells and ancient wizards, hung above the desks. And a cache of scrolls sat in a maple cabinet, beneath a sheet of thick glass.

Kellach leaned over the largest worktable at the back of the room, inspecting something on the desk.

"Nothing seems out of place, Kellach," Driskoll said as he padded up behind his brother. "Maybe Zendric just stepped out for a few minutes?"

Kellach looked up and gave Driskoll a smirk. "Not exactly, Driskoll. Take a look at this."

Kellach picked up a gnarled charcoal pencil from the worktable and held it out with a triumphant look on his face. The wooden stick was only about two inches long, and it seemed to be covered with bite marks.

Driskoll scoffed. "So what? It's just an old pencil."

"Oh, right." Kellach took in a quick breath. "I forgot you're not an apprentice."

Kellach whispered a few words under his breath. When Driskoll looked back at his brother's hand, the pencil had sprouted tiny silver wings. It lifted off of Kellach's palm and hovered for a moment. Then, it zipped in front of them, tracing a message in silver writing through the air.

Dear Apprentices,
An urgent matter has called me out of the city. I do not expect it to require more than a few days of my time. I have

prepared lessons for each of you. You will find your assignments
in your study chambers. I expect you all to have made significant
progress on them by the time I return.

Until then, you know where you're allowed to go and where—
and what—to stay well away from. I would deeply regret having
to rescue, free, or transform you back to your normal self should
any of you disobey me. You could find yourself regretting it even
more deeply than I, however.

I trust you and expect you to cooperate with one another.
Remember: Discipline, devotion, and diligence are the keys to
success, and not just in wizardry.

If any of you need assistance, seek out Kellach. He knows
almost as much as he thinks he does.

Until I return,
Zendric

As soon as Driskoll had finished reading, the words dissolved
in a shower of silver glitter. The sparkles fluttered to the floor
and instantly disappeared, like melting snowflakes.

" 'He knows almost as much as he thinks he does.' " Driskoll
chuckled and looked up at his brother. "That's a good one."

"I'm sure he meant it as a compliment," Kellach said brusque-
ly. "I *am* his best student, you know." Kellach whirled around and
marched over to his study chamber. He pulled out his chair and
sat down, studying a piece of parchment from the top of the pile
of work on his desk. "This is an advanced spell." Kellach looked

up triumphantly. "See, I told you I was his best student."

Driskoll rolled his eyes. "Can't studying wait for a second? What about the sign? What are we going to do now?"

Kellach shook his head as if to clear it. "You're right." Kellach rubbed his chin thoughtfully. "You know, if Zendric isn't here, that means his study is free to explore." Kellach smiled. "Maybe we can find some answers in one of his books!"

He crossed the room confidently, heading for the stairs at the back wall that led to the second floor. When Kellach reached the staircase, he let his hand rest on the postcap of the handrail, a carving of a ruby-eyed snake, fangs extended. He looked back at his brother. "Well, are you coming?"

Driskoll crossed his arms. "Are you sure that's a good idea? Doesn't Zendric forbid you from entering his private study? We could just ask him when he gets back."

Kellach sighed. "He may forbid his *regular* students from entering his study, but I'm his best student. And we're Knights of the Silver Dragon, remember? If we don't figure this sign out, something's going to happen to Dad. I'm sure Zendric won't mind."

Driskoll shrugged. "Okay, but I'm telling him it was your idea when he yells at us." And with that, he followed his brother up the stairs.

At the top of the stairs stood a tall ironbound door. This door, too, stood ajar. Driskoll was sure he could hear a rustling sound in the room beyond.

"Did you hear that?" he whispered. "I think someone's in there."

Kellach nodded. "There's only one thing to do," he whispered back.

"Right. I'll go get Dad." Driskoll turned to run back down the stairs, but Kellach grabbed him by the arm.

"No." Kellach pulled his brother up the stairs and pushed him through the door. "We go inside."

CHAPTER

11

Zendric's private workspace seemed immense to Driskoll. The ceiling was nearly ten feet tall. A huge plush carpet, midnight blue and embroidered with constellations, covered the wood floor. Near the window, stood a massive oak desk. The room smelled musty, like an old library.

Shelves overflowing with massive, leather-bound books lined one of the walls. And there, beneath the bookshelves, sat a woman, her nose stuck in a book. The two boys exchanged a puzzled look.

Kellach cleared his throat. "Excuse me," he said.

The woman looked up and literally jumped to her feet. "Oh! I'm sorry. I didn't hear you come in. I was so busy reading." The woman held up the book in her hand. "I found a delightful story called *The Iliad*. It's by a Greek writer. Perhaps your brother would enjoy it too." The woman brushed a stray brown curl out of her face, tucking it behind her ear, her *pointed* ear. Driskoll realized she was an elf, and suddenly he recognized her.

"I know you." Driskoll said. "You're Selden, the city librarian. You helped me last year with my 'Bards through the Ages' report."

Selden clasped her hands together and jumped up and down. "Oh yes! What a brilliant project that was." The librarian looked like she was barely older than a teenager, but that was impossible since she'd been working in Curston for seventy-five years. Maybe all that nonstop reading kept Selden young, Driskoll thought. It must be true, because there wasn't a wrinkle anywhere on her face nor a gray hair among her glistening dark brown, long wavy hair.

"Zendric mentioned in his note that you boys might stop by." The librarian thumbed in the direction of Zendric's desk by the window. A gnarled wooden pencil much like the one downstairs lay in the center of the oak desk. "You must know that he's been called away, right?"

Kellach nodded. "But what are you doing in Zendric's private study?"

"Oh! He didn't tell you? Zendric asked me to come by to assist him with some research. In his note, he asked me to return next week, but I couldn't resist taking a sneak peek at his collection."

"Well, I guess you can be going now," Kellach said, hoping that Selden would go away so they could get to work, snooping.

"Oh, I meant to . . . but then I got lost in this amazing book.

I just can't put it down." Selden's eyes twinkled whenever she talked about books.

Kellach's face fell. With Selden in the room, there was no way they could get away with silently browsing Zendric's collection. Selden registered the look.

"You know, boys," Selden added, "I have to tell you, as a librarian I feel a little out of sorts today. If only I had some type of research challenge before me." Selden sighed. Her eyes were still twinkling, and her sigh couldn't disguise the good humor in her message to Kellach. "I'd hate to waste a day of research just because Zendric is away," she added.

Driskoll sensed that this good-natured librarian could be trusted. He elbowed his older brother and whispered, "Ask her about the sign!"

But Kellach was one step ahead of his brother. "Hmmm . . . maybe I can think of a challenge for you," Kellach said.

"Great!" Selden said. "Bring it on."

"Okay, let's see what you can find about a sword and serpent symbol, drawn in charcoal. It looks something like this."

Kellach handed the librarian the sketch he had made. "Now, this particular symbol has appeared at crime scenes where magic may be involved."

"Intriguing. Yes, indeed, an intriguing symbol," Selden said. "Is the symbol magical? Or was it created by a magical creature?"

"I'm not sure," Kellach admitted. "I was hoping you could

help me find that out. I mean, that is part of your challenge. Could you find reference books that might shed some light on this mysterious symbol?"

Selden closed her eyes. When she opened them, they glistened with excitement. She stood in front of the bookshelves and slowly turned in a circle, pointing at books here and there, summoning them to fly off the shelves and head toward her. The books started their flight quickly, hurling like a catapult, but as they neared the middle of the room, they'd slow down and gently float down to Selden's arms, gathering themselves in two tidy little piles. The piles grew taller and taller. The librarian placed them on Zendric's desk.

"That should do," she said to Kellach. "Now, if you'll excuse me, I need to return to my reading. I'll be in the far corner, lost in a book, completely oblivious."

"Thank you, Selden," Kellach said.

"Oh, but thank *you* for giving me a challenge today, Kellach," the librarian said, and then she seemed to disappear among a pile of books.

Kellach and Driskoll stood by Zendric's desk, each in front of a different stack of books, and set to work.

CHAPTER

12

"These books have better titles than contents," Driskoll said wearily, after looking all the way through *Incredible Sightings of Magical Symbols*. He yawned and shut the book, releasing a puff of dust into the air.

He was struggling to stay alert. Driskoll had gone through nine large, musty books. Most of the volumes looked as if no one had opened them for a century or so. He'd found information on other magical signs, but nothing that was an exact match—or even a reasonably close match—to the one across from the wainwright's shop and the other crime scenes.

If only Moyra were here, Driskoll thought, this work would go twice as fast. Then he remembered their fight earlier that morning. He sighed. Moyra was his friend. His best friend, really. He probably should apologize to her.

Maybe Kellach was having better luck with his stack of books. Driskoll leaned back in his chair and glanced over at his brother.

The older boy sat nestled deep in Zendric's leather armchair, leafing through a book that looked as thick as a stack of ten normal books. Every now and then, the apprentice wizard murmured excitedly like he was making some great discovery. Then he stuck his nose back in the book and continued reading.

Maybe Kellach was saving all the juicy, truly magical books for himself, Driskoll thought. He didn't know whether Kellach would really do that or, whether he did, if it would be to save the good stuff for himself or to protect Driskoll from stumbling across some secret magical information. Driskoll shook his head to drive those thoughts out of his head—and to wake himself up.

Briiinnnggg.

Driskoll nearly fell off his chair, startled by the sound of the entryway chime. Someone was waiting at the front door of Zendric's tower.

Driskoll stood up and stretched. "I'll go see who it is."

"Hmmm-mmm," Kellach said, deeply involved in his reading.

Driskoll slipped through the ironbound door, headed down the stairs and across the first floor of the tower.

Slowly he opened the huge front door.

But there was no one there.

He stepped out on the stoop and looked all around the yard, still holding the doorknob.

"Hey," a voice came from the tall tree flanking the doorway.

Driskoll nearly jumped off the step he was standing on.

Moyra dropped to the ground in front of him.

"Moyra! What in the gods' darkest names are you doing up in that tree?"

She shrugged. "I was hiding, just in case Zendric answered the door and he didn't want visitors. You know how he gets . . . "

"Well, you nearly scared the skin right off of me."

"Sorry," said Moyra. "I mean, sorry I scared you like that. Not sure what else I would be sorry about." Moyra looked sheepishly at the ground.

"Look. I'm sorry for what I said earlier, Moyra," said Driskoll. "You are a thief. But you're an exceptionally good, extraordinary, super, stellar kind of thief. A good thief, if there is such a thing."

Moyra scowled.

"I-I mean," Driskoll stuttered. "Can we just forget this whole thing?"

Moyra hrumpfed. "I guess there's a chance that an imposter could have attacked Latislav," she said, picking up a twig off the ground. "I realize now that some things are . . . are not as they seem . . . " She started tracing shapes with the twig in the dirt. She looked up. "Although the attacker did look exactly like your dad."

Driskoll could feel his face flush red. "Why do you have to be so stubborn? Can't you give my dad the benefit of the doubt, for once?"

"I am!" Moyra threw up her hands.

"Liar!" Driskoll turned his back to her, crossing his arms.

Moyra reach out and put her hand on the younger boy's shoulder. "Seriously, Dris, I want to believe your dad is innocent. But if the guy who attacked Latislav wasn't your dad, who was it?"

"It was the Trickster," said Kellach, from behind them.

"The Trickster?" Driskoll spun around.

Kellach came out of the front door of the tower and closed it tightly behind him. "I found a book by one of the old Knights of the Silver Dragon, a wizard by the name of Griffin. Chapter 13 tells about a meeting he had, right here in Curston, with a being that called itself the Trickster."

Driskoll asked, "Does the wizard mention anything about the sign?"

"He doesn't say so specifically, but look what I found tucked inside this book." From the back of the thick volume, Kellach pulled out a piece of parchment. It was covered in a fine layer of dust, and the edges were pocked and discolored. Kellach lifted it up for all of them to see.

The fragile parchment held a small drawing at its center. And though the ink had browned and smeared with age, there was no mistaking the upright sword and twisted snake. It was the same symbol that they had spotted outside the Grinning Hippogriff, Latislav's home, and every recent crime scene in Curston.

"That's how I knew I was on the right track." Kellach explained.

Driskoll looked like he might burst. He was practically hopping from foot to foot in excitement.

Kellach rolled his eyes. "Okay, okay. You can go ahead and say it . . ."

"I knew it!" Driskoll said. "I knew it! I thought of it first! And I told you but you didn't believe it."

"Okay, now that you're done gloating, I can tell you what Griffin wrote," Kellach began. "According to this book, the creature has been to Curston several times. Each time it's here, the creature causes as much trouble as it can and implicates an innocent person for the crime. Then the Trickster leaves town, and the people it framed are left to pay the price for its pranks and damage."

"Are you sure we can believe this Griffin guy?" asked Moyra. "I mean, why would he know so much about the Trickster? Maybe he wasn't telling the truth."

"According to Zendric," Kellach said patiently, "Griffin was one of the most honest Knights there was."

Driskoll looked back at the tower. "Zendric? How do you know? Is Zendric back?"

Kellach chuckled. "No, Zendric wrote the introduction to the book." Kellach leafed through the book to the front page and turned it around for them to see. "See? Here, Zendric explains that he chose Griffin to write this book because he was considered such an honorable man."

Kellach shut the book and wrapped his arms around it, his face serious again. "It seems that the Trickster isn't just a character from a silly old nursery rhyme. It's real, it's deadly, and it's back."

"How did this Knight—what's his name, Guffin?" asked Driskoll.

"Griffin," Kellach corrected.

"How did *Griffin* find all this out?" Driskoll asked.

Kellach held up the book and turned to chapter 13. "According to this, Griffin and some other Knights were investigating a crime spree in Curston, just like we are. One night, Griffin was patrolling Broken Town by himself. After searching for hours, he decided to take a break in a tavern. And there, sitting alone in a corner, was the Trickster, staring at him."

"Hang on," Driskoll said. "How did Griffin find the Trickster? The Trickster is a shapeshifter, remember?" Driskoll began to sing the old nursery rhyme:

From dwarf to elf
To babes in arms
He'll change his shape
To do you harm

"Yes," Kellach droned. "You were right about that too. According to Griffin, the Trickster can take the shape of anybody it watches—even for a little while."

This time Driskoll didn't say "I told you so," but he couldn't wipe the grin off his face. "So, presumably, the Trickster would have assumed someone else's form in the tavern that night. Then how could Griffin have recognized it?"

"Griffin was a wizard," Kellach said, as if that explained everything.

But Driskoll and Moyra looked at him blankly.

"He cast a spell, of course," Kellach said the words slowly and loudly as if he were conducting a lecture. Kellach relished any chance he had to prove the depth of his wizardry knowledge. "This spell allowed Griffin to see the Trickster in its true form. It's called a true sight spell. And it's very advanced. Only a wizard of great powers can perform it."

"Does a shapeshifter like the Trickster have a form of its own? What does it really look like?" Moyra asked.

Kellach scanned the chapter until he came to the right passage. "Here Griffin says it didn't look either distinctly male or distinctly female." He put his finger on the page and moved it across the print as he picked out the details. "It had long, gangly legs and arms, green eyes, and was skinny to the point to the point of being gaunt. It was hairless, and Griffin says its gray skin was like clay. He also says it had a 'blank, featureless' face."

"No features? As in, no nose? No mouth?" Driskoll smiled. "That's so creepy."

"It's disgusting," said Moyra. "And impossible. I bet that it was just Griffin's way of saying the Trickster didn't show any emotions or feelings."

"According to what Griffin wrote," Kellach continued, "the Trickster said it could assume the shape of almost any person it had seen even for a few minutes. Griffin said that for a moment, while they were talking, the Trickster even took on Griffin's appearance, and then it went back to the way it looked when Griffin first entered the room."

"So what happened once Griffin found the Trickster at the tavern?" asked Driskoll.

"Listen to this." Kellach began reading from the book:

The Skinned Cat was quite crowded that evening. There was a spot at the Trickster's table, but I waited for it to invite me over. It motioned to me and I sat down with my mug of ale. I was feeling rather pleased with myself for having tricked the Trickster, but then it said in a low, gravelly voice, 'I see that you, my good wizard, can see me all too well.' Its manner was calm and almost teasing. We began to talk and continued talking for nigh three hours.

"Did Griffin ever find out why the Trickster was causing so much trouble?" Driskoll asked.

"That was the first question he asked. The Trickster told him that a member of the ruling council had hired it. This man wanted to be magistrate and he was willing to do anything to be chosen for the post. So he paid the Trickster to create trouble all around town. The plan was that the then magistrate would be blamed for the crimes and would be asked to step down. Soon after that, the Trickster would leave town, and the new magistrate could claim to have ended the rash of crimes."

Driskoll took in a breath. "Do you think that's what's happening to Dad?"

Kellach lifted his head from the book, nodding. "Or something like it. Someone must have hired the Trickster to impersonate Dad and make him look like a criminal."

"Who would do such a thing?" Driskoll asked. "And why?"

"I'm not sure. Dad does have enemies. But I can't think of anyone who would do something this despicable." Kellach scrunched his mouth to one side and rubbed his chin, deep in thought.

Moyra was uncharacteristically quiet. She sat down and hugged her knees to her chest as if she were cold. Her eyes skimmed the people on the street outside Zendric's tower.

"It's possible your dad isn't the only one the Trickster's impersonating," she said, her voice nearly a whisper.

"What do you mean?" Kellach cocked his head, confused.

Moyra's eyes were pleading. "Promise you won't tell Torin?"

Kellach looked insulted. "Of course."

"Promise?" Moyra insisted.

Kellach lifted one hand. "On my honor as a Silver Dragon."

"Okay." Moyra let out a big sigh. "I saw my Dad in Main Square today, only he was acting so strange." She was talking fast, as if she wanted to tell her story before she could change her mind. "He stole something that he wouldn't even normally want—a big fat fur-lined coat—but he did it in a clumsy way, like he wanted to be seen and be caught."

"That doesn't sound like Breddo," Kellach admitted.

"He didn't act at all like himself. He was running faster than I'd ever seen him run. And even though he was trying to get me to follow him, he wouldn't wait for me."

"Was he arrested?" Driskoll asked.

Moyra shook her head and squeezed her legs tighter. "No, he was running so fast no one in the square could keep up with him. But that's not the strangest part." Moyra gulped. "When I went home, my dad was there, asleep in the bedroom! My mom said he's sick and that he'd been sleeping all day. At first it didn't make any sense. But now I understand. That wasn't my dad in Main Square." She looked at Driskoll. "It was the Trickster."

Driskoll had been listening to Moyra's tale with a frown on his face. When she finished, he crossed his arms and glared at her. "Why didn't you tell us before?"

"I was embarrassed . . ." Moyra hung her head. "After everything I said about your dad. I'm sorry. Plus I was scared you'd tell your dad."

Driskoll's expression softened.

"Do you think my dad's in danger too?" Moyra asked quietly.

"I doubt it," Kellach answered. "The Trickster is simply expanding his campaign against Dad. A simple crime, performed in broad daylight, yet the watch is powerless to stop it.

It's almost worse than impersonating Dad. It makes him look incompetent."

Driskoll and Moyra nodded.

"But it's probably no accident that the Trickster picked the image of your father as its disguise," Kellach continued. "The Trickster must know we're onto it. Moyra, you've seen the Trickster twice—once at Latislav's house and again in the market. You've really got to be careful."

Moyra, who usually would admonish Kellach for treating her like she couldn't take care of herself, nodded sullenly.

"I know. I'm thinking the same thing. But it's not just me who needs to be careful," Moyra said looking at first at Kellach, then at Driskoll. "If we're right, the Trickster could be after each one of us. We're all in danger now."

CHAPTER

13

Everyone was quiet for a minute. Driskoll finally broke the silence.

"If the Trickster is truly a shapeshifter, we'll never know when we're around it," Driskoll said. "It could be anyone, anywhere. It could even be . . . YOU!" he shouted at Moyra.

"Cut it out, Dris." She sounded annoyed. "Things are creepy enough around here without you acting crazy. Because the truth is, it could be . . . YOU!" Moyra shouted it back in his face.

"Cut it out, both of you," Kellach scolded them. "Seriously. Driskoll does have a point. The only way we can be sure we're safe is if we create some kind of test, something that we can use to prove to each other that we are who we say we are."

"Like what?" Driskoll asked.

"Well . . . " Kellach leaned against the tower wall. "The Trickster can take on the shape of any person, but the impersonation only goes skin deep. It doesn't know anything about the person like thoughts, feelings, and past experiences."

Moyra snapped her fingers. "I've got it. Let's ask each other questions that only we three know the answers to." She turned toward Driskoll. "You go first."

"Okay." Driskoll looked to the sky, tapping his foot. Then suddenly, he whipped around, staring Moyra directly in the eye. "Okay, Moyra. Where's the secret entrance to Watchers' Hall?"

Moyra scoffed. "Too easy! It's in Broken Town, on Snickle-bark Way. Okay, my turn. I've got a hard one." She gave Driskoll a haughty smile before turning to Kellach. "Kellach, who made Locky?"

"Ssarine, the medusa," Kellach answered instantly. He turned to Driskoll. "Driskoll, what's the creature you fear the most?"

Driskoll suddenly looked nervous. He began tapping his toes again. "Um . . . goblins . . . No, zombies! . . . Wait, no, . . . goblins. Goblins."

Moyra and Kellach looked at each other and at Driskoll. Then they both burst into laughter.

"What's so funny?" Driskoll asked.

Kellach patted his brother on the shoulder. "Are you SURE about that Driskoll?"

"Yeah! Goblins? Wait . . . " Driskoll's eyes went wide. "Don't you believe me?"

Kellach chuckled. "We do . . . we do . . . Okay, now we'll

also need a code word in case we ever doubt each other again," Kellach said.

"How about *Griffin?*" suggested Moyra.

"Excellent idea," said Driskoll.

"Agreed." Kellach nodded.

"A tougher question is how to find the Trickster," Moyra said.

"Not to mention how to keep it from taking on the shapes of Dad, Breddo, or other people and getting them in trouble," Kellach said.

"What did Griffin do to stop the Trickster?" Driskoll asked.

Kellach lifted the book up again, scanning the pages.

"Griffin eventually persuaded the Trickster that it should leave Curston immediately. The wizard seems to have been quite powerful. He convinced the creature that it wouldn't be able to survive against the combined power of the Knights. Together, they would be able to destroy its true essence." Kellach looked up. "I'm not sure what he means." He shrugged and went on. "In return for its confession, Griffin offered to give the Trickster one day to leave town before telling the rest of the Knights about his discovery. He also agreed not to use any spell or gem to find it."

Driskoll wanted to ask what kind of spell, but Kellach was in one of his rare storytelling moods. Usually it was Driskoll who liked the captive audience to listen to his tales. Driskoll knew enough to remain silent and just let his brother keep talking.

"The next evening, Griffin told his fellow Knights all about the Trickster—and who had hired it. A few of the Knights were upset with the wizard at first, not trusting the Trickster to keep its word. But the rash of crimes ended, and the Knights easily captured the man who had hired the Trickster and turned him over to the watch. Griffin's friends later hailed the wizard for ending the threat to Curston with nothing more than a conversation."

Driskoll clapped his hands together. "Okay, so all we have to do is find this Trickster and give it a piece of our minds, just like Griffin did."

Kellach and Moyra both looked at him.

"Right?" Driskoll added quietly.

Kellach shook his head. "It's not that simple. The Trickster can take on any shape. There's no way we will be able to find it."

"Can't you use the same spell that Griffin did so that we can find the Trickster and see its true form?" Driskoll asked.

Kellach puffed out his chest. "I'm sure I could . . . But . . . But I'd need Zendric's help," he admitted. "It's a very difficult spell and I don't know exactly how to do it. It's not in any of my spellbooks."

"Well, I don't know about the rest of you, but I'm not going to give up," Driskoll said boldly. "I'm going to find that Trickster."

"And how exactly do you plan on doing that?" Moyra asked.

Driskoll squatted down on the step, with his head in his hands. Then suddenly, he sat up straight. "Kellach, didn't you say something about a gem? That Griffin promised not to use a spell or a *gem* to find the Trickster?"

Kellach took in a quick breath and began leafing through the book again. "You're right. It's called a seeing gem. It works in a similar way as the spell. But I've never seen one before."

Driskoll opened his mouth, but before he could speak, Kellach cut him off.

"Before you ask, the answer is no. Zendric doesn't have one. At least I don't think he does."

"Is there anyone in Curston who would have one? Could one be made?" Moyra asked.

They all knew the answer to that one. If Zendric didn't have a seeing gem, there wasn't a chance that anyone else in the city would. Zendric wasn't just a wizard. He was known as a master of wizardry and magic. The top resources for magic in Curston were all within the confines of Zendric's tower and Zendric's brain.

Driskoll slumped down again, his chin resting in his palm. After a few minutes, another idea popped into his head.

"Hey!" Driskoll said. "Remember last spring when that musician, that bard, came to town? Dad took us to see him perform."

"Sure, so what? That bard didn't have any magical powers," Kellach said, rather dismissively.

"Maybe a bard doesn't need magical powers," Driskoll said. "Because a bard spreads wisdom through songs and stories. This particular one sang a song about a warrior who had to find the person who had killed his lady love."

"And?" said Kellach, waiting for Driskoll to get to the point more quickly.

"Well, luckily for us, *this* bard"—Driskoll thumbed at his own chest— "meaning *me,* remembers that in the song the killer was invisible. The ghost of the warrior's love came to him in a dream. She told him he had to find the eye of a monster called the attavus. The eye would allow him to see everything as it really was. So the warrior went to a cave and fought the attavus. Then he took its eye and used it to find the killer."

Moyra leaned closer. "Was the attavus supposed to be green, with a round body like a giant pumpkin, stringy tentacles, and a mouth filled with sharp teeth?"

Driskoll took in a quick breath. "Yes! How did you know? Did you hear the story too?"

"Not exactly." Moyra grinned wryly. "Last winter, my dad tried to search for treasure in the Dungeons of Doom. He didn't get very far, though, because he met up with a terrible one-eyed creature. It lives somewhere near the bats' lair. It hunts bats, I guess."

Kellach recoiled, but Driskoll leaned closer. "Wow," said Driskoll. "How did your dad make it out alive?"

Moyra shrugged. "He can run like a demon when he needs to." Moyra looked directly at Driskoll and Kellach, her eyes shining. "Daddy didn't tell me the name of the creature, but he did say the creature's eye glowed like a gem. It's possible that it could be the seeing gem, isn't it, Kellach?"

"Maybe. But a bard's story and the tale of a known thief aren't much evidence to go on." Kellach sighed. "Still, it's all we have. I say we go for it. All in favor?" Kellach raised his hand for a Silver Dragon vote.

Moyra's arm shot up, but Driskoll wasn't so hasty. His mind flashed back to the goblins and the owlbear from their last adventure in the dungeons. He wasn't exactly looking forward to meeting those creatures again, but he'd do anything for his dad. He raised his hand.

"Great! Then it's settled," Moyra said. "We'll need equipment, lights, rope, and stuff," she glanced up at the sky and the dark storm clouds up above, "and waterproof packs. If that storm breaks, we'll definitely need waterproof gear."

Driskoll held up his palms. "Hang on. We can't raid Dad's closet again. He was steaming mad after the last time."

"Don't worry. I know where to get everything we might need." Moyra seemed chipper now.

Kellach nodded. "It will take me a while to get some things out of Zendric's tower that might help us."

"It might take me a little time, too," Moyra said. "I'll meet you by the Westgate at noon. Dris, are you ready for Round Two of your lesson in stealth and thievery?"

"You bet!" Dris said. "At the very least, you can use me as your pack mule to haul everything back here. Oh, curse it . . .

what about Dad?" He turned to Kellach.

"He's on duty all day. He'll never know we aren't at home."

"Right. But that also means we have to make sure he doesn't see us or hear about us heading out to the ruins," Driskoll said.

"You guys need to learn to stick with me more often," Moyra said. "I know how to evade the careful eyes of the watch. Come on, Dris!" She was already down the steps of Zendric's tower and heading toward the square. Driskoll quickly fell in step beside her.

"Moyra, I guess I was wrong before," Driskoll started to say.

"You bet you were!"

"And I was right too," Driskoll said huffily. He made himself take a deep breath before he continued. "The thing is, we were both right and we were both wrong."

Moyra nodded.

"It wasn't my dad who attacked Latislav," Driskoll said, "but you saw what you saw. The Trickster made you believe it was my dad, and there's no reason why you would doubt your own eyes. That Trickster certainly is good. But the mistake I made was when I called you a liar. You know I don't think that."

"I do know that," Moyra said. "We're in this together now. You, Kellach, and me. We have to trust each other."

"Griffin." Driskoll held out his hand.

"Griffin," Moyra repeated, and the two of them shook on it.

CHAPTER

14

Moyra and Driskoll sped across Curston until at last they reached their destination: a little house next to the low wall separating Broken Town from the Wizards' Quarter. The building was a mere shell of its former self. All the windows were shattered, and large chunks of wood were missing from the walls. There was no door, only the rotted remains of a tilted doorframe.

Moyra held out her hand, palm up, her eyes darting all around the area. Then she waved Driskoll forward, leading him around to the side of the house.

Driskoll picked his way over broken boards, glass shards, and overgrown weeds. The side of the house nestled against the edge of the crumbling wall. He found Moyra standing in front of a large rock in the wall that looked as though it weighed a hundred pounds. She leaned over and began tugging on the edge of the stone block.

"What are you doing?" Driskoll asked. "We'll never be able to move that thing. It looks like it weighs a ton."

"That's where you're wrong." Moyra grunted as her fingers dug into the crevices in the giant rock. "The real piece of this wall was removed years ago by a couple of thieves in the guild. This one is made of wood and plaster, but it fools most folks."

"What is this place?" Driskoll looked over his shoulder at the crumbling house behind him. "It looks like a dump."

Moyra laughed. "That house, my friend, is the most top secret bolt-hole in all of Curston."

"A bolt-hole? You mean a place thieves use to meet and to stash their stolen goods, right?" asked Driskoll.

"Yes, but how do *you* know what a bolt-hole is?" Moyra gave up her battle with the rock and stared at Driskoll. She sounded not only surprised, but a little peeved.

"Hey," said Driskoll, "Kellach may be the smart one, but I'm the one who listens when people talk. Dad knows about some of these, but he thinks that not letting on that he knows—and not letting the thieves guild know that he knows—might be handy."

"Hmmm. You dad is smart. I can see where Kellach gets it," Moyra said with a smirk. Driskoll swatted her lightly, although he knew she was egging him on.

"Well, I'm sure your dad doesn't know about this one." Moyra looked at Driskoll. "And you'd better not tell him."

Driskoll held up his hand. "On my Silver Dragon honor."

Moyra nodded. "This bolt-hole may look like an abandoned house from the outside, but underneath lies a storage room, a locked treasure room, and a room for meetings. And under this stone," Moyra grunted again as she tugged harder on the rock, "lies the secret entrance."

"Help me here," Moyra continued. "This rubble isn't as heavy as stone, but it's pretty cumbersome. With the two of us, though, we should be able to move it quickly. It tilts back like this."

She pointed out a cleverly hidden set of hinges beneath the fake piece of rubble.

"How'd you find out about this rock?" asked Driskoll as he sidled up to Moyra and grabbed hold.

"How do you think? My dad. He told me a story one night about two sisters he knew about five years ago. Their names were Maria and Maggi. The two sisters robbed an evil merchant—"

"Which merchant?" Driskoll interrupted.

"I can't remember his name. Nimo? Something like that. Anyway, can I finish the story?"

Driskoll nodded.

"So, this merchant used to cheat his customers, most of whom were poor folk from Broken Town. The merchant was powerful, and the two sisters knew that the watch wouldn't do anything to stop him. But they wanted revenge. So they stole his gold, and built this place to store it. After a year, they returned all the gold to the merchant's victims. It's Broken Town justice."

"Wow, I didn't realize thieves could be so generous," Driskoll said.

Moyra scowled.

"I mean, I didn't know so many of them could be as generous as you are," he hastily added. "Did Maggi and Maria ever get caught?"

Moyra shrugged. "That's the strange thing. The two sisters are some of the worst thieves around. But for some reason, the watch never arrested them. Of course, the merchant was furious, but there was nothing he could do. He would have had to explain why he'd had all that gold in the first place, and he wasn't about to admit the truth."

"Maybe my dad realized what the merchant was up to and he decided to let Broken Town justice prevail."

Moyra gave Driskoll a sideways glance. "Doubtful." She tugged harder on the stone. "Come on, keep tugging on this thing."

"Does anyone else know about this place?" Driskoll asked as he pulled the stone.

Moyra nodded. "Sure, most of the thieves in town. But I'm sure there's no one here," answered Moyra. "Thieves don't tend to use places like this in broad daylight. All we need to do is slip inside and head for the storage room. There we'll find rope, lanterns, lamp oil, waterproof packs—everything we'll need to go back into the dungeons."

With a giant creak, the fake stone finally pulled away,

revealing a hole in the hollow wall. Driskoll stuck his head in the hole and looked down. A ladder led down to the damp earthen floor below.

"Let's go!" Moyra said.

Moyra and Driskoll climbed down the set of rusty iron rungs to the floor at the bottom of the tunnel. They remained there for a moment, listening for any noise and waiting for their eyes to adjust to the darkness.

"Okay," Moyra whispered, "we'll follow the wall here on our right for about ten or fifteen feet until it comes to a secret door in the bolt-hole." Moyra led the way down the passage feeling the wall with her right hand.

When the duo reached the end of the passageway, Moyra pressed her ear against the wooden door that led into the bolt-hole.

She reached for the doorknob and pushed the door gently.

The door opened a crack, and Moyra slid her eyeball up to the slit, peering inside. She pulled her head back.

"The coast is clear," she whispered, and then she swung the door open.

Driskoll looked over Moyra's shoulder. He saw a dark corridor with only one fluttering torch in a wall sconce giving a faint light. The floors here were made of flagstones, and there were doors on either side of the passage about halfway down and another door at the far end. From the door on the right came light and the sounds of a conversation.

"I thought you said there wasn't anyone down here during the day," Driskoll said in the softest whisper he could manage. "Now what?"

"You stay here," Moyra whispered. "I'll go down the hall to the far door. That's the storage room. I'll get what we need and come back."

"I think we should stick together," Driskoll said, his voice shaking a bit. "I mean, there's so much stuff that I should help you carry it," he quickly added.

"If even one of those thieves catches a glimpse of the captain's son down here, they'll have my head."

" I can be sneaky, too, you know. I've learned from the master. And the faster we're in and out of here, the better, right?" Driskoll still whispered, but he added a brave tone to belie any of his fears at that moment.

"All right. But if we're spotted, Dris, you have to run. Get Kellach and your dad and tell them what happened. They won't hurt me once they know who my dad is."

"Deal. But we're not going to be spotted," Driskoll said. He hurried through the open space into a short hallway. Moyra came through after him, shutting the door behind her with a quiet click.

After looking cautiously down the hallway, Moyra put her fingers to her lips and motioned Driskoll to follow her. They would have to go right past the meeting room to get to the storage area and then come back past it again, this time carrying all their supplies.

At the middle doorway, Moyra sidled up against the wall and froze. The door was open about two feet, more than enough for someone inside to see the kids go past, if he or she was looking at the right time. Driskoll wondered how Moyra would decide what would be the right time to move. He watched her and saw her pull something out of a pocket of her vest.

It was a small piece of highly polished steel. Driskoll recognized it as a gift from her dad for her eleventh birthday. He'd seen her use the reflective metal as a small mirror. Now he watched as Moyra positioned it so she could see around the corner and into the room. A handy tool for a thief. A handy tool for today, too.

Moyra held the steel mirror close to the ground, moving it until she had an adequate view into the room. Several people sat around a rickety old wooden table on equally rickety chairs. Luckily, none of them was seated in a spot where they had a full view of the dim hallway where the kids crouched.

Driskoll saw her put the small mirror back in her vest, take a deep breath, and dart across the opening, stopping just beyond the doorway to listen. No one within the room reacted. They were all talking, and no one seemed to notice any movement. He waited for her signal, and then he did his best to imitate his friend.

Whew! Both of them had made it.

Moyra and Driskoll moved down the hall to the storage area's door. It was unlocked. They opened the door slowly and slipped inside, leaving the door just slightly ajar behind them.

"First," instructed Moyra, "find a lantern and some oil so we can see in here. Then we can close this door."

Driskoll rummaged around, quickly finding a lantern with a tad bit of oil in it and a bit of tinder. He took out his flint and steel to make a spark, and then lit the lantern. With the light of the lantern available, Moyra closed the door tight behind them.

"All right," she said, "we'll need more oil for that lamp, another lantern, three waterskins, and a grappling hook, in case we have to climb. I have a set of lockpicks, in case we need them."

She hadn't needed to add that. Driskoll would have found it noteworthy only if Moyra hadn't had her lockpicks with her. He'd wager that she even slept with the things.

"Dris, we also need a crowbar, just in case. Oh, and waterproof packs." Moyra pointed to the shelf above their heads. "They're up there."

A couple of minutes later, they had most of the gear loaded into their knapsacks, along with a third one stocked for Kellach. They put their packs on, blew out the lamp they'd lit, and moved to the door. The sound of the conversation in the meeting room hadn't changed, so they entered the hallway, closing the door gently behind them.

They moved back to the doorway to the meeting room. Moyra checked again with her mirror and moved across the opening.

Driskoll hefted his pack over his shoulder and waited for the signal. In one hand, he held the pack they'd planned to give to Kellach. His arm already ached from carrying it. He rested it on the floor.

Moyra checked her mirror one more time, and then she crooked her finger. "Now," she mouthed.

Driskoll lifted the heavy pack off the floor by the top strap and tried to move quickly but softly. He was so busy trying to keep his footsteps quiet that he didn't notice the grappling hook dangling out Kellach's pack. Just as he crossed in front of the doorway, it slipped out and clanged against the stone floor.

The room of thieves fell silent.

"Did you hear that?" a voice growled. "There's someone out there."

Heavy footsteps thundered across the floor.

"Run!" Moyra whispered through clenched teeth as she started racing down the hallway. Driskoll swept the hook off the floor and wasted no time in following her.

They hurtled down the passageway, through the door, and into the tunnel. Driskoll took the ladder two rungs at a time. He burst out of the hole in the wall aboveground, falling flat on his face. He picked himself up and kept on running.

Once they were several streets away, Moyra slowed to a walk, and Driskoll caught up with her.

"Sorry, Moyra. I-I . . . I didn't see that hook."

Moyra looked back at him, her expression stern. "You have a lot to learn about being a thief, Driskoll."

Driskoll hung his head and nodded.

Moyra continued, "That was lesson three: how to escape from a pack of rival thieves." Her face broke into a grin. "You passed."

Driskoll's head snapped back up. "You mean you're not mad?"

Moyra laughed. "Nope. Come on. Kellach's waiting." And with that Moyra began racing toward the Westgate.

It was all Driskoll could do to keep up.

CHAPTER

15

Kellach was leaning against the city wall a few feet down from the Westgate when Driskoll and Moyra arrived at last.

"What's the plan?" Driskoll handed his brother the pack they had stocked for him. "How are we going to get through here without any watchers noticing us and telling Dad?"

"Keep to the shadows and they'll never even see us." Kellach pulled something out of his robe pockets and slipped it into the rucksack. Then he slung the bag over one shoulder and began walking. "The watchers are much too busy to notice three innocent kids."

Kellach cocked his head in the direction of the three men guarding the gate. The watchers were busy questioning an entering merchant. Although the man was carrying nothing more than a burlap sack, the watchers had him pinned against the wall and were firing questions at him. The man looked terrified.

"They're suspicious of newcomers these days," Kellach whispered to his brother and Moyra as they slipped through the gateway and onto the winding road beyond.

Fallen leaves, soggy from the morning's rain, littered the road to the ruins. There was no sound between them as they walked, except the noise of their boots splashing through the shallow puddles that covered the road.

Driskoll's thoughts floated to the last time they had attempted to enter the infamous Dungeons of Doom. The area had swarmed with goblins—vicious little creatures who seemed intent on capturing the three kids, or worse. Driskoll shivered and unconsciously rested his hand on the sword at his belt.

"Kellach?"

The older boy looked back at his brother, surprised to hear a voice.

"Yeah?"

"How are we going to get past the goblins?"

"Not to worry, little brother," Kellach said. "Zendric told me that the goblins are nearly gone from the ruins these days. The owlbear killed off most of them. The remaining goblins turned on the goblin king. I'd hazard a guess that there are hardly more than a half dozen down there. Nothing that my magic and your sword can't handle."

Driskoll grinned, and stood up a little straighter. But Moyra scowled.

"Don't get too cocky," she said. "Those creatures are like

roaches. They'll be back before you know it, meaner and hardier than ever before."

The three kids hiked on in silence until at last they came to the fallen city's legendary bronze gates. Vines and other plants snaked up the gateway. Driskoll pushed to the front of the group. From there he could clearly see the ruined clock tower that marked the square and the main entrance to the Dungeons of Doom. He scanned the old city. He didn't see any goblins. But how could they be sure?

"What are you waiting for?" Kellach said as he confidently jogged through the bronze gates and the city beyond. Driskoll shrugged and followed him.

As they neared the edge of the city's old plaza, Kellach padded up behind a low crumbling wall. Moyra and Driskoll crouched behind him. They peered over the fallen blocks of stone.

Roughly fifty yards across in each direction, the plaza was a mere shadow of what it had once been, back when the city was the richest town in the region. Now it was nothing more than a gateway for adventurers, who entered the Dungeons of Doom, hoping to capture some of the riches that lay below this once thriving city. More often than not those adventurers never returned.

A splashing sound caught Driskoll's attention. Driskoll's eyes flew to the center of the square and a stone basin, surrounded by a circle of crumbling statues. Once a bubbling fountain, it was now nothing but a shallow basin ringed by headless and armless figures.

The splashing sound came again. This time Driskoll could zero in on the direction of the noise. It was coming from the fountain, for sure, somewhere behind the statue of a woman. She was draped in a toga, but both arms and half of her head were missing. Even from this distance, Driskoll could see a thin, muddy puddle in the center of the ruined fountain basin. But from this angle, he couldn't see behind the statue.

His whole body went tense. He looked back at his brother.

"Maybe we should—" he began.

But Kellach was already on the move. The apprentice hopped over the low wall and marched to the center of the square, his hand reaching inside his belt pouch for some spell components.

The splashing grew louder. Moyra put her hand on Driskoll's shoulder. "We've got to help him," she whispered. "Come on."

Driskoll drew his sword, and the two followed Kellach. When they reached the statue, Kellach held his hand up for them to halt behind him. He peered around the stone figure.

With an ear-splitting squeal, a tiny creature, no bigger than a squirrel scurried out from behind the figure. Driskoll caught sight of gray fur and a hairless tail. The creature raced across Kellach's foot.

"Ah!" Kellach shouted. He jumped up on the nearest stone block and stood there, quivering. "What was that?"

"It's just a rat!" Moyra said. The three kids watched as the rat raced across the plaza and disappeared into a crevice of one of the crumbling stone buildings surrounding the square.

Kellach shivered. "Ew. I hate rats." He stepped back onto the ground.

Driskoll sat down on the edge of the fountain and started to giggle, softly. Moyra flopped down next to him, making no effort to hide her laughter.

"Did you see the look on Kellach's face?" Moyra said between giggles. "He looked like he was about to collapse into tears . . . He battles goblins, and owlbears, and medusa. But give him a rat . . . " Moyra couldn't finish because she was laughing so hard.

Kellach pressed his lips into a flat line. He looked at Moyra. "I don't like rats, okay?"

Moyra just laughed.

"Come on, get up," Kellach said as his eyes darted around. "It looks like the area is all clear. Let's get down to the dungeons."

He marched forward and stood at the top of the stairwell in the center of the square. The stone steps cut into the floor of the crumbling plaza, leading down into the shadowy dungeons below. Kellach pulled a lantern out of his pack and lit it. Then he looked back at Moyra and Kellach. "I'll go first to scope it out. As soon as I give the okay, you two follow me."

Moyra and Driskoll nodded silently. And with that, Kellach slipped down the stairs.

Perhaps it was the fit of laughter, or perhaps it was the relief of seeing a rat and not a goblin. Whatever it was, for some reason, Driskoll felt, for the first time in two days, that everything was going to be all right. They would get the eye, find the Trickster, prove their father's innocence, and send the shapeshifter on its way. It wouldn't be easy, but they could do it. He breathed a sigh of relief.

Not thirty seconds later, Kellach came hurtling up the stairs, without his lantern. When he reached his brother and Moyra, he skidded to a halt and leaned over, grabbing his knees and panting.

Moyra and Driskoll looked at him, their eyes wide.

Boom. Boom. A regular noise, like the beat of a giant drum, echoed from deep inside the stairwell.

"What? What is it?" Driskoll asked.

"Well . . . the good news is. . . it's not a goblin . . . ," Kellach panted.

Boom. The noise was coming closer.

"What's the bad news?" Driskoll asked.

But Kellach didn't have a chance to answer.

From the shadowy recesses of the stairwell, a huge figure emerged. It looked something like a goblin—with yellowish skin and pointy torn ears. But it was, by far, the biggest, hairiest goblin that Driskoll had ever seen. It stood more than seven feet tall on two gigantic legs, rippling with muscles. A tiny brown pug nose, much like a bear's, sat below two angry red eyes. Long sharp fangs poked up out of wide meaty lips. Coarse brown hair covered its entire body and most of its face, the long strands hanging in a tangled mess from the bottom of its square jaw. Chains looped around its broad chest. They clanked as the creature walked up the stairs and stepped into the light.

As the thing caught sight of the three kids, it lifted its arm and shook its fist. Then it stepped forward, prepared to charge.

CHAPTER

16

W hat is that thing?" Driskoll shouted as the three kids plummeted across the ruined plaza.

"It's a bugbear!" Kellach said. "It's related to the goblins, but it's bigger and meaner."

The ground shook as the bugbear gave chase.

"And faster!" Moyra added. "There's no way we're going to outrun that thing! We need a plan."

"Just let me think for a second," Kellach began.

"Too late!" Moyra screamed.

Driskoll looked over his shoulder and skidded to a halt.

The bugbear had grabbed Moyra by the back of her jacket and was pinching it between two fingers, holding her high off the ground.

"Unhand me, you disgusting freak!" Moyra shouted.

Her legs kicked the air, trying desperately to gain some advantage against the giant creature. But it was no use. The bugbear merely laughed, a roaring, frightening sound.

It raised her higher and scanned her up and down as if trying to determine the tastiest place to take its first bite. A stream of drool trickled from its fat lips. It opened its mouth revealing hundreds of sharp long fangs.

"Nooo!" Driskoll rushed forward, his sword raised. He swung at the creature's stumpy legs. Each blow left a thin trace of blood on the creature's calves. But as strong as his blows were, they seemed to have no effect on the monster. The bugbear registered each blow much like the bite of a mosquito, which is to say, barely at all. It lifted its leg and swatted the boy away. Driskoll sailed into the air and landed a few feet away.

"Quick, Kellach! Cast something!" Driskoll shouted. "It's going to eat her!"

"I'm thinking!" Kellach called.

"Moyra," Driskoll called. "Don't give up."

Moyra wriggled frantically. As she moved, her pack, still hanging off her shoulder, slipped down to the crook of her elbow. She reached inside and her hand wrapped around the first thing she found: her waterskin. She lifted the fat sack of water out of the pack and slapped it against the creature's biggest tusk.

It burst like a water balloon all over the bugbear's face.

With an agonized roar, the creature recoiled. In an instant, its fingers released Moyra and its hands went to its face. Moyra dropped to the ground.

Whimpering, the bugbear stepped back.

Moyra laughed triumphantly. "Hah! Take that, you freak!"

Suddenly Kellach was in motion, racing back across the square.

"Quick, you two!" he shouted. "Get to the fountain!"

"Are you crazy?" Driskoll said. "The fountain's practically right next to that THING's front door."

"I'm serious. Come on! I have a plan."

"Well, it's about time," Moyra said, already plummeting across the square.

"Hey, wait for me!" Driskoll hopped to his feet and took off after her.

By the time Moyra and Driskoll reached Kellach, he was standing in the fountain basin, staring hard at a crumpled piece of parchment in his hand. Driskoll recognized it immediately as the parchment Zendric had left Kellach on his desk.

"Okay, Kellach, what now?" Driskoll asked. Driskoll danced from foot to foot, trying not to let the shallow puddle in the fountain soak through the soles of his boots.

But Kellach didn't answer. He was too busy reading, his lips whispering the words as he scanned the parchment in his hand.

Driskoll looked out across the square. The bugbear was shaking its head frantically, like a dog who had just emerged from an unwanted bath. Drops rained off the creature as it desperately tried to dry its face. At last satisfied, it crouched low and slowly scanned the plaza until its eyes locked on Driskoll's stare. It muttered something in Goblin that came out sounding like a growl.

"Kellach!" Driskoll leaned over and shouted in his brother's ear, "Are you cracked? This is no time to do your homework. We've got to get away from that thing!" Driskoll jabbed his finger frantically in the direction of the bugbear.

Kellach shook the parchment in Driskoll's face. "This isn't just homework. Give me a second. I need to concentrate." Kellach put his finger on the parchment and peered at it closely.

The ground began to shake as the bugbear came closer. What had sounded like a growl from yards away grew into a full-fledged roar.

"Any time now, Kellach!" Moyra said.

The bugbear was within a few feet of them now. It was so close Driskoll could see it licking its lips and smell its stinking breath.

"Should we run?" Driskoll shouted, looking over his shoulder then back at the bugbear. "I think we should run!"

Moyra crouched low, her fists clenched, ready to race off at Kellach's word.

"No wait." Kellach said. "You'll see."

Still staring at the paper intently, Kellach reached down and dipped a finger in the muddy puddle at the bottom of the fountain's basin. He whispered a few words under his breath and then traced a pattern in the air.

Suddenly, Driskoll's feet began to feel wet, really wet. He

looked down and saw the puddle rising, first inching up the sides of his soles, then splashing over the tops of his boots, until finally it reached up to his knees. What had once been a mere muddy layer of water was now a sparkling clear pool. Every few seconds, a thin stream of water squirted out of the crumbling fish at the fountain's center.

"Yes! Kellach cried, doing a little jig in the water. "I did it! That was an advanced spell too. Zendric thought it would take me all week to get it. See, I am his best student."

Driskoll looked at his brother, puzzled. "I don't get it."

"Look!" Kellach smiled smugly and pointed at the bugbear. The creature was backing up and whimpering quietly. The vicious grin on its face had been replaced by a look of pure fear. It circled the fountain but did not dare to come closer.

"Hah! I get it!" Moyra said. "That big fat bully is scared of water! And therefore, it's scared of us!" Moyra bent over and swept the surface of the now full fountain, splashing a wall of water at the bugbear. "Take that!"

The bugbear cried out and jumped back, but it didn't escape the cascading wall of water.

Kellach nodded. "When you threw your waterskin on the bugbear, I realized that fear of water was that creature's one weakness. And then I remembered the spell. Zendric thought it would take me all week to get it."

"You just said that." Driskoll rolled his eyes.

But Kellach grinned smugly. "Pretty good, huh? I guess I

work best under pressure." Kellach crossed his arms and leaned against a statue of a man with one arm.

"So what are we going to do now?" Driskoll asked. "It doesn't look like that thing is going to leave any time soon."

The bugbear was still circling the pool and glaring angrily at the three kids.

Moyra shrugged. "Eventually it'll get bored." Her eyes lit up. "Or maybe we just get it to run away." Moyra swept the surface of the pool and sent another wave crashing over the bugbear. The creature muttered something in Goblin and stepped farther back.

Driskoll laughed and quickly joined in the fun. With each splash, the bugbear retreated farther. Soon Driskoll and Moyra were as wet as the bugbear and laughing hysterically.

"This is great!" Driskoll shouted. "All we have to do is splash it until it runs away. Right, Kellach?"

There was no answer.

"Kellach?"

Driskoll looked back to where Kellach had been leaning against the statue. A small circle of swirling ripples marked the spot where he once stood.

But Kellach was gone.

CHAPTER

17

"Gods!" Driskoll cried. He looked at Moyra then back at the ripples on the surface of the pool. "Where did he go?"

Moyra lifted her shoulders. "Maybe he made himself invisible?"

Driskoll shook his head. "I don't think so. We'd still be able to talk to him. And we'd hear him. Kellach? Are you there?" There was no answer. Driskoll looked back at Moyra. "I don't even think he knows that spell yet."

Driskoll lifted his hand to his forehead and peered intently across the open plaza. "Do you think he could have made a break for it across the square?"

"I doubt it. We would have seen him."

"Kellach! Kellach!" Driskoll called as he sloshed through the pool, moving along the edge of the circular basin. He peered off into the distance, scanning the crumbling buildings one by one. But there was no sign of his brother.

When Driskoll had made a full circle, he found Moyra squatting near the spot where Kellach had disappeared. She was sweeping her hand beneath the surface of the pool and staring intently at the water.

As Driskoll approached, she stood up and shook the water from her hand. "You're not going to believe this . . . " she began.

"What?" Driskoll asked.

"I think there's a . . . a tunnel down there."

"What do you mean, a tunnel?"

"Tunnel's the wrong word. It's more like a pipe, or a drain. When Kellach did that water spell, he must have triggered the plumbing. I think there's a pipe down here, draining the water from the pool. See? "

Moyra grabbed Driskoll's hand and put it close to the ripples that still danced on the surface of the water. Driskoll could feel an invisible force tugging at his fingertips. He jerked his hand away.

"Gods! That's strong! You think Kellach got sucked down by that thing?" Driskoll peered down at the water. He could almost make out a dark hole, about as wide around as a small barrel, beneath the surface. He looked back at Moyra. "Do you think he"—Driskoll gulped—"made it?"

Moyra shrugged. "There's not enough water to completely fill the pipe. I could feel an air hole when I put my hand down there. It's possible that he just slid down to the old sewer system beneath the city."

"Okay." Driskoll adjusted the pack on his back, pulling himself together. "Well, then, we'll just have to go after him."

Moyra nodded. "There's just one problem."

Driskoll lifted his eyebrow. "Yes?"

"If I'm right, the drain leads directly to the Dungeons of Doom. And there's no telling what's down there. I don't know anyone who's entered the dungeons this way."

Driskoll took a deep breath. "We'll have to risk it. We've got no choice. We have to go after him. He might be in trouble down there."

Moyra nodded. "I thought you'd say that." She sat down in the water and scooted forward until her shoes touched the edge of the ripple. "See you on the other side, Driskoll!" Taking a deep breath and holding it, she slid into the center of the whirlpool.

"Wait! What about the bugbear?"

But Moyra couldn't hear him. Driskoll watched as first her legs were sucked into the blackness. In an instant, her torso followed. Moyra looked up and waved at him as her head went under. And then, she was gone.

Driskoll risked a look at the bugbear, which was now leaning forward, its eyes wide. It was clearly terrified by the sight of children disappearing in the pool of scary water.

"Boo!" Driskoll shouted.

The bugbear gave one final whimper and then went racing off into the ruined buildings beyond the plaza. Driskoll laughed to himself. Thank the gods. At least they could get down below without having to worry about running into that creepy creature again.

Driskoll sat down in the water. The pool was icy cold and he shivered as he positioned himself in front of the tiny whirlpool. Pinching his fingers tightly around his nose, he took in a deep breath, and with a silent prayer to St. Cuthbert, he pushed himself forward into the swirling drain.

CHAPTER

18

"Aaaahhhhh!" Driskoll couldn't hold back his screams as he plummeted down the steep pipe.

Just as Moyra had suspected, after sliding into the opening of the drain, his head emerged from the water and he could breathe easily. He unclamped his nose and used his hands the best he could to slow his ride down the slippery pipe.

But it didn't do much good. The pipe was covered in slimy green moss. Water trickled from behind him with just enough force to propel him down the chute.

Driskoll sat up, and his fingers scrambled for some place to grab hold. But the more he tried to reach out and slow his descent, the more it hurt. His backside bumped painfully against the old iron surface, and his fingers scraped against the sides.

Finally he gave up.

He held his arms flat against his sides and leaned back,

hoping to get down as quickly as he possibly could.

The pipe twisted and bent at odd intervals, sending him sliding up one side of the chute and then the other. At one point, he reached a flat area. He had to sit up and dig his heels into the water, scooting forward over the next edge.

Then his stomach dropped out from under him, and once again, he was sliding.

At last he saw a dim light at the end of the tunnel. He shot out of the end of the chute. For a brief second, he was flying through the air, and then with a splash, he plunged into a pool of murky water.

He swam to the surface and emerged, coughing. After rubbing the water from his eyes, he looked around, instantly catching sight of Moyra and his brother up on a ledge above him. Their clothes were rumpled and soaking wet. But they were both smiling.

Kellach leaned over and held out his hand to pull his brother out.

"Was that fun or what?" He smiled.

Driskoll gave a halfhearted grin. "I guess you could call it that." He hoisted himself out of the river of muck, using his brother's hand as leverage. He stood up on the ledge, next to Moyra and shook the water from his body.

Driskoll took in a deep breath. There was a distinct change in the air. It was musty and smelled of rotting plants and garbage. The murky water flowed in a straight channel below him, through a stone archway and into the shadows beyond. The light from Kellach's lantern reflected off the river casting a weird greenish glow on the cavern's ceiling.

Behind them, just beyond the ledge, another small archway led to some sort of tunnel. It had smooth walls, and flagstones lined the floor. Large wooden ceiling beams supported the tons of dirt and rocks.

Kellach swept his hand toward the tunnel. "Welcome back to the Dungeons of Doom, Driskoll." Kellach smiled. "We are far past the goblins' territory and within minutes of the attavus's lair. This is all going exactly as I had planned."

Driskoll looked at Moyra and rolled his eyes. Moyra smirked back at him, but she didn't say anything.

"Now, before we enter the dungeons," Kellach said, "I want to prepare you for our mission." Kellach reached into his ruck-sack, pulled out two small bags, and handed them to Moyra and Driskoll.

"Moyra, that pouch has two stones. Each one is enchanted to emit a loud bang when you throw it at something. Do not, I repeat, do NOT throw a stone unless I tell you to."

Moyra opened the pouch and fingered the two small, smooth stones.

Driskoll had already opened his bag, only to find two smaller bags inside.

"Dris, each of those small bags is full of a sticky liquid that gets thick like glue when it's exposed to the air. It's good for throwing at the feet of anyone you want to slow down. I've kept the two most dangerous bags for myself."

"What's in them?" asked Moyra, already impressed with Kellach's knowledge about these strange items.

"I hope you won't ever need to know," Kellach said ominously.

Driskoll tucked the bags into his pocket and squeezed the last of the water out of his jacket. Then he looked at his brother. "Well, what are we waiting for? Let's get going!"

Kellach led the way, holding Moyra's lantern. Moyra followed him, and Driskoll came last. When they reached the point where the tunnel narrowed, they halted. Kellach kneeled down on the rocks adjacent to the crawl space and shone the lantern's light through it.

"It looks like this opens into a passageway that goes left and right. Hold this, Moyra," he said, handing her the lamp. "I'll crawl through first. Then you two come on through." All three of the Knights wiggled through the hole.

They had followed the passage for more than a hundred feet when it opened into a chamber of worked stone. Driskoll noticed splintered remains of tables, chairs, and cots. In the corner of the room, several empty barrels leaned haphazardly against the wall. The room looked like an old guards' chamber from back when the city above had once thrived.

Kellach strode across the room toward the doorway on the other side. Moyra and Driskoll tiptoed behind him, but no sooner had they reached the center of the room, than a rustling sound came from the corner. Kellach lifted his hand to call a halt, and they all stared at the barrels.

Out of the corner came two of the largest rats Driskoll had ever seen.

They were as big as small horses, their hairless tails as thick as a grown man's arm. The big creatures sniffed the air, eyed the three kids, and lumbered toward them, chattering all the way. The noise sounded like fingernails scraping the chalkboard.

Driskoll realized in an instant that the rat they had met in the fountain must have been one of their babies and that could mean only one thing. He shivered. There were more of them.

"Run!" shouted Driskoll.

But Kellach stood frozen. His eyes were as wide as saucers, staring at these larger-than-life rat nightmares.

Moyra took one look at Kellach and threw up her hands.

"Oh for the gods' sake!" she said as she set down the lamp. Moyra stepped past Kellach and pulled a stone from her pocket, hurling it at the floor in front of the rats.

The stone struck the flagstone floor directly in the path of the rats. A booming crash, as loud as thunder, filled the room. The three kids all clutched their ears and cowered from the sound. The rats fared much worse.

The sound struck the rodents almost like a physical force. So close were they to where the stone hit, and so accurate was Moyra's throw that the stone even hit one of the rats on the nose as the rock bounced.

The giant rats screamed at the pain and ran away in a panic.

"Great shot, Moyra!" shouted Driskoll. He could tell he was shouting but he couldn't stop himself. His ears were still ringing from the force of the sound. Driskoll shook his head and wiggled a finger in an ear, trying to stop the ringing.

"Why'd you waste the stone?" demanded Kellach. "I was going to cast a spell."

Moyra scoffed. "Uh-huh. Right after your knees stopped shaking?"

Kellach looked at the ground and muttered, "I told you I didn't like rats."

▮ ▮ ▮ ▮ ▮

They continued their journey through the hallway. The corridor now ran straight a long way before turning so far right that Driskoll realized they were walking in the exact opposite direction from which they had started.

They walked on—the passage bearing them this way and that. They spoke little. Often the only sounds they could hear were their own breathing and their footsteps. The trio passed several more side passages and small rooms. Yet there was no sign of the attavus.

The corridor turned again.

"Hey, you two, I think we're going up hill," Moyra said. "We'll be heading toward the surface again. And I'm not sure if that's good or bad."

"For finding the attavus, it's probably a bad sign," answered Kellach. "If the attavus spent much time near the surface, more people would report seeing it."

"Shush," said Moyra as they approached a large chamber. "Do you hear something? It sounds to me like . . . squeaking."

"Aww, not more rats," Kellach said.

"I don't think it's rats, but we'd better check it out," Moyra said as she quickened her pace into the room. Kellach and Driskoll aimed the light of their lanterns to each side, and top and bottom of the huge chamber.

Now the noise seemed to bounce off the walls. A horrid, putrid smell filled their nostrils. It came from a big pile of a white goo on the far side of the room.

"Turn off your lamps! Or at least cover them!" Moyra urged. "I think there's a light coming from somewhere else." Kellach extinguished his lantern, while Driskoll hid his light under his jacket for a moment.

"You're right, Moyra. It looks like there's a crack in the wall up there," said Kellach pointing above the stinking pile.

"What else is up there? I think I see something moving," said Driskoll.

"Let's find out, shall we?" quipped Moyra, sounding sarcastically optimistic. She picked up a small rock and threw it high and far in the general direction of the light.

Suddenly, the room erupted into a screeching mass.

"Bats!" shouted Driskoll as thousands of the creatures flew toward him.

"Ah!" Kellach began yelling almost as loudly as the bats. His arms swept in front of him. Driskoll pulled him down, and Kellach quickly covered his head.

Driskoll watched the spectacle guardedly through his fingers.

The black cloud of shrieking, panicked bats moved throughout the chamber a few times and then turned and flew out the exit high up on the far wall, fleeing the source of the disturbance.

"Sorry about that," Moyra said.

Kellach lifted his head. "The only thing I hate more than rats are bats." He sighed. "But this is good."

"Good?" Driskoll asked.

"The attavus hunts bats, remember?" Kellach explained. "This means we must be close."

"Uh, Kellach," Moyra said, "I think we're even closer than you think. Look!" Moyra pointed at the room's entrance.

A creature, with a body as big around as a barrel, lumbered through the passageway. Its one eye shone an evil green, and it moved on five of its ten long tentacles as it came into the room. It growled a deep, hungry sound as it prepared to attack.

CHAPTER

19

I t's the attavus!" Driskoll shouted.

Kellach jumped to his feet, whispering a stream of magical words. His hands moved in an intricate pattern until at last he pointed at the attavus.

A finger-thin stream of ice lanced across the room striking the attavus on its barrel-like body. It hissed and screeched in pain—a sound worse than that made by all the bats combined.

The attavus was hurt, but not deterred. It turned and used its ropy tentacles to grasp the chamber wall. Pulling itself up onto a ceiling beam, it hung from four tentacles directly above Kellach, Moyra, and Driskoll.

"Spread out," Kellach instructed as he dodged a tentacle that tried to slap him to the ground. "Don't let those things touch you."

Two tentacles lashed at the young wizard. Kellach side-stepped one and ducked beneath the other.

"I don't think it's after us!" Driskoll shouted to his brother. "It wants the one who attacked it. It wants you!"

One tentacle struck a hard slap across Kellach's chest, knocking him backward. Then the other wrapped around the apprentice wizard's legs and began to lift the boy in the air.

"Kellach!" Driskoll threw himself at Kellach's legs and grabbed hold with one hand.

With the other, he drew his sword and started hacking at the tentacle, the blade biting deeply into the pulpy flesh. At last, he cut through the tentacle, and Kellach dropped to the ground.

"Thanks," Kellach muttered as he wobbled to his feet. He struggled to catch his breath, and Moyra grabbed Kellach's robes to help him stand.

"Forget about the eye!" shouted Driskoll while they all dodged another tentacle. He pointed at the entrance to the room. "We have to get out of here!"

"No," Kellach wheezed. "This way." He pointed into the darkness.

"Are you cracked?" Driskoll asked. "We'll be trapped!"

"Trust me."

The three kids raced across the chamber, just barely escaping. Swinging its tentacles out ahead of it, the attavus moved across the ceiling and climbed partway down the wall to pursue its quarry.

Small, horrible-smelling pellets flew all about the trio as they raced to reach the place near where the bats had been roosting.

As the group neared the far side of the chamber, the light shed by Driskoll's lamp also revealed an opening on the far wall.

"Don't say it." Driskoll looked over at his brother. Kellach smiled.

They went as fast as they could toward that doorway. They found themselves in a passage that led uphill. At the far end shone a dim light.

Driskoll looked back over his shoulder. "Keep moving," he said, "it's still after us."

"Hand me the lantern," Kellach whispered. "I need to see where we're going."

"You two watch out ahead. I'll keep an eye out for Mr. Tentacles," said Driskoll.

The corridor was much like the last ones they had entered. Wooden beams lined the passage at regular intervals, supporting the walls and the dirt ceiling.

The farther Moyra, Kellach, and Driskoll ran, the narrower the passage became. Every once in a while a sprinkle of soil rained down on them. Soon they had to walk in a single file, at a crouch.

Driskoll kept looking over his shoulder. He was certain he could hear the attavus snaking along behind them.

Soon, Kellach called a halt.

Driskoll looked ahead and with a sinking heart, he said, "It's a dead end."

"Not quite," Kellach said as he pointed upward. "Look." About ten feet above them, a vertical passage led to a large iron grate. Light filtered through the thick bars.

"I'll climb up," Moyra volunteered. She leaned her back against the wall and lifted first one foot, then the other, onto the wall directly in front of her. In this precarious seated position, she began to inch herself up the wall.

"Hurry, I can hear it coming," urged Driskoll anxiously.

Moyra reached the top of the vertical passage as fast as she could.

"The grate's stuck! I can't move it," Moyra called down. "What do we do now?"

"I can hear the attavus!" called Driskoll. "It's almost here."

"Stay calm, Driskoll," said Kellach. "I have a plan. Moyra, tie some rope to the grate and get down here. If this is going to work, it'll take all of us."

A length of rope fell to the floor near the boys, and seconds later Moyra appeared, shimmying down it.

"What now?" Moyra asked. "Have you got another spell?"

"None of my remaining spells will hurt it. But, if we time this right . . . Get out that stone I gave you."

Moyra fished it out of the small cloth bag in her pocket.

Just then, the attavus appeared in the pool of light cast by Driskoll's lantern. With four of its tentacles, the monstrous creature dragged itself forward. There were now only four crossbeams left between the three kids and the end of the passageway.

The three Knights backed up against the far wall.

"Driskoll, get out a bag of resin," commanded Kellach. "And wait until I give the word."

"Okay." Driskoll pulled one of the bags out of his pocket without taking his eyes off the attavus.

"Don't throw the stone until I tell you, Moyra," Kellach said.

"Got it," she replied.

The attavus crept its way closer to the trio. As it reached the third crossbeam, the monster stretched two of its tentacles up to the ceiling. It gripped the wooden beam and pulled itself even closer.

"Now, Driskoll!" Kellach shouted.

Driskoll hurled the bag of sticky resin.

The bag hit the beam between the attavus's tentacles and, with a wet splash, spread goopy liquid all over the monster's limbs. The attavus screeched and tugged its two tentacles. But they were stuck fast to the crossbeam.

"Yes!" shouted Driskoll. He looked over at his brother for a hint of approval. But Kellach's gaze was fixed on the vial clenched in his right palm. The small glass bottle was filled with fiery red liquid.

"Let's see how you like this," Kellach muttered. His head whipped up and he shouted. "Hold on, you two. Things are about to get ugly." Then he launched the vial up in the air. The uneven ceiling and the force of Kellach's throw sent the vial skittering along the ceiling. The bottle did not break until it struck the third ceiling beam. With a whooshing roar, flames erupted over much of the beam and the struggling attavus.

The beast again uttered its weird cry of pain. Its free tentacles waved frantically above it to ward off any more flames.

It tried again to free its stuck tentacles. It grasped the side beam with a third tentacle and pushed frantically. But the sidebeam dripped with sticky resin, and before long, the third tentacle was stuck fast, too.

Kellach then launched his second and last vial of liquid fire. It struck just beyond the side beam.

Driskoll smiled at his brother. "Good shot!" He watched the fires burn and the attavus pull even more frantically to free its limbs, bracing its remaining free and healthy tentacles against the wall.

"Do I throw this stone now?" Moyra shouted over the sounds of the crackling flames and the screeching creature.

"Not yet," Kellach answered.

"So what do we do now?" she asked him.

"We wait and see."

"If that thing pulls any harder on that beam," Moyra shouted, "the whole tunnel will collapse."

Kellach looked at Moyra. "Exactly."

"But how are we supposed to get out if that monster collapses our only way out of here?"

"Don't worry." Kellach smiled. "I have a plan. Just watch."

The attavus was near panic now. The resin held its tentacles firmly and a fire blazed just a few feet above its head. Like most creatures, it had an instinctive fear of fire. This fear lent strength to its efforts, and the creature had managed to pull the side beam a few inches out from the wall.

The flaming crossbeam began to sag. Small rocks and streams of dust cascaded down from the ceiling. The more the attavus pulled to free itself, the faster the soil above rained down. The monster pulled, tugged, and strained for its life, its long cry reaching higher and higher pitches.

"Now! Moyra!" Kellach shouted. "Throw that stone right between the beam and the attavus."

"I can't," said Moyra, turning her head from the scene and covering her ears with her forearms. "Isn't there a way we can end its misery quickly, mercifully?" she asked.

Kellach turned to her. "Mercifully? You want to give that monster mercy? Two moments ago, it would have happily eaten us all for supper. Maybe you'd have preferred to watch it kill Driskoll and me rather than watch this. Besides, it's not dead yet, and until it is, we're still in danger. Now throw the stone!"

Moyra took a deep breath and threw the stone. Her aim was true, and a tremendous bang shook the narrow tunnel.

The attavus completely panicked. It tried to recoil from the sound, pulling so hard on its stuck tentacles that it tore one free, leaving half of the limb still stuck to the beam. Dark green blood poured from the ragged end. As the monster writhed, its wounded tentacle sprayed its blood up and down the corridor. The blood reached as far as the end of the corridor, splattering Kellach, Moyra, and Driskoll's faces with dark green liquid freckles.

"Ew!" Moyra cried as her hand flew to her face. "That's disgusting!"

The attavus gave one last, panicked pull. And then it was over. The crossbeam promptly cracked, split, and fell to the tunnel floor, bringing over a ton of rock and earth directly onto the monster.

Its cry was lost in the crash and tumble of boulders.

CHAPTER

20

Clouds of dust filled the tunnel. Coughing, Driskoll wiped his eyes and tried to survey the damage.

Kellach said, "Don't move too much for a few minutes, or you'll just kick up more dust." He punctuated his point with a sneeze.

"Come on, Kellach," said Driskoll, "let's get out of here before any more of the tunnel collapses."

"Leave? We can't leave," countered his older brother, "We don't have what we came for yet."

Kellach walked toward the pile of rubble that, somewhere beneath it, concealed the attavus.

"I see one of the tentacles," said Kellach, motioning the others closer. "It's still stuck to this part of the beam. Help me find the body. I hope the eye survived the collapse."

After several minutes of digging, they found the battered corpse of the attavus. Its round body was facedown.

"Be careful," whispered Moyra. "Make sure it's dead before you reach your hand down there."

Kellach stopped as his hand was about to grab the green carcass.

"Here. I'll do it." Moyra drew her dagger from its sheath and plunged it into the back of the monster's round body. The attavus didn't move. It didn't even twitch.

"Thanks," said Kellach as he again reached to turn over the carcass. The creature's body didn't seem to have any bones. The whole thing was made of the squishy tissue. Up close, its eye looked like the eye of a cat. It appeared to be undamaged.

"We'll have to cut it out." Moyra leaned forward. Driskoll watched as she sliced the eye out of the socket, trying hard not to retch.

Moyra handed the slimy ball to Kellach, with her head turned away. "Quick! Take it! Before I throw up."

Kellach wrapped the eye in a small drawstring pouch that he took out of his pocket. Then he slipped the pouch into his pack.

"We have the eye," Moyra said. "Can we go now?"

"The tunnel's blocked the way we came," said Driskoll.

"Somebody please tell me how we're going to get out of here," said Moyra.

"Well," Kellach said, "I was going to ask you to do this, but Driskoll is smaller to begin with, so it has a better chance of working if he does it."

"Does what?" she asked.

"Just watch." With that, Kellach closed his eyes and brought to mind the words and gestures of a spell.

Soon, Driskoll, stood less than one foot tall.

"Hey!" the mini Driskoll squeaked, stomping his tiny foot. "Why'd it have to be me!"

"I told you," Kellach said. "You're the smaller one to begin with."

Driskoll crossed his teeny arms and sighed, sounding no louder than a gentle breeze. "Fine. Now what am I supposed to do?"

"You climb!" Kellach leaned over and hoisted his brother onto the rope hanging from the ceiling. Driskoll scrambled up the rope to the grate above. He squeezed between the bars and wriggled out onto the surface.

Driskoll looked around. He was standing on some narrow street of the ruined city. The light was still bright in the afternoon sky. They had been gone only a few hours. It seemed like days.

Driskoll looked up one side of the roadway and then down the other. But there was no sign of goblins, bugbears, or any other creatures.

"It's all clear up here," Driskoll squeaked down to his brother. "Now change me back! I don't like being this short."

Driskoll could hear his brother muttering an arcane word. In the blink of an eye, he was his normal size again.

"Use the crowbar to lift the grate!" Moyra called from below.

Driskoll reach into his pack and pulled out the long iron rod. He wedged the thin curved end underneath the edge of the grate. He pushed the bar down and with a loud creak, the grate swung free.

Driskoll untied the rope from the top of the grate and retied it around a large column on the other side of the street. Then he tossed the other end down the open hole.

Moyra was out of the hole in an instant.

Kellach took a bit longer to scale the rope, but at last he heaved himself onto street level. He stood up slowly, trying in vain to dust off his apprentice robes. His clothing was covered in mud, dirt, guano, and attavus blood.

Driskoll waved his hand in front of his nose and backed away. "Pew! You stink!" A smell worse than rotten eggs, spoiled milk, and dog poo combined wafted off Kellach's body.

Kellach smirked. "So do you, little brother!"

"We all do," Moyra said, looking down at her own gray clothes, caked in dirt. She looked up at the sky. "Come on. We'd better get back to Curston, before your dad calls out the infantry."

"Dad will kill us if he sees us like this," Driskoll said.

"You can clean up at my house," Moyra said already marching ahead.

Both boys smiled their thanks, and the trio raced through the ruined city, onto the Westgate and Moyra's cozy home.

CHAPTER

21

Moyra opened the door to her family's small cottage in Broken Town and beckoned Driskoll and Kellach inside.

Driskoll gave her a look as he tiptoed inside. "Will your parents mind if we're here? I know your mom doesn't like us much."

"Don't worry," Moyra said. "My dad's probably still asleep, but he's a sound sleeper." Moyra glanced around the small front room. "And it looks like Mom's still at work in the market. They'll never know you were here. Just keep it down, okay?"

The brothers followed her into the cottage and over to the tiny kitchen. Moyra bustled about, getting a fire started in the cooking fireplace. An iron kettle hung from the hearth, directly over the small fire. Moyra filled the kettle with water from the boys' waterskins.

There was a rustle on the other side of the bedroom door. "Dad, it's just me, don't worry!" Moyra called softly toward the closed door. The boys held their breath. "I got in a bit of a scrape and I need to boil some water to clean up," Moyra added.

"It's Moyra," Breddo said from the other side of the door. Driskoll held his breath.

But he sleepily added, "Wake me if you need me, baby." It sounded as if he were going to go back to sleep.

Moyra winked at the brothers.

"What do we do with this eye?" Driskoll asked.

Moyra glared at him. "Shhh! Let me get something to clean up with first." She whirled around to grab a towel, but as soon as she turned, she froze in place.

Moyra's mother stood in the doorway, her arms crossed. "I thought I heard voices. Did you bring the boys here to hide?"

"Mom!" Moyra said. "I thought you were still at the market."

"I came home to check on your father." Royma stepped back and closed the bedroom door gently behind her. "He's still dead to the world," she said to Moyra.

Driskoll noticed an uncharacteristic look of worry in Moyra's eyes. "It's only an expression," Royma added.

"We just need to clean up," Driskoll said quickly. "Dad will have a fit if he knows that we went down—er—I mean, that we got so dirty."

"You haven't been down to the ruins again, have you?" Moyra's mother asked, her eyes narrowing.

All three kids smiled weakly.

Royma held up her hand. "I don't want to hear about it."

Royma stared at Moyra. "You're worse than your father, with his high-falutin' ideas about making easy riches down in that dungeon . . . "

Royma shook her head. "But at least you're home safe. In fact, it might have been safer to have been where you were than to be on the streets of Curston today." Royma clucked her tongue. "And boys, I think your whereabouts are of little concern to your father right now. He seems to have other things on his mind." Her lips tightened.

"Mom, what is it? What happened?" Moyra asked.

Royma sighed. "The watch might as well take over every little thing in Curston, the way those idiots are behaving these days. The whole town is abuzz about watchers acting as if they owned every shop, every pub, even everyone of us. It's all anyone could talk about at the Skinned Cat today. In fact, one watcher, a quite young man, I might add, came into the Skinned Cat and helped himself to a leg of lamb and two pints of cider."

"Maybe he was going to pay later," Driskoll said, not really believing his own words.

"Pay later?" she screeched. "I don't think so! He grabbed the meat right off the plate of Riley Skarsoff, he did. Took the two pints off a tray that the barmaid was carrying. She nearly lost everything else on her tray, she was so surprised by what he'd done. She called him by his name, as if she knew him. Yet he just laughed as she stumbled and nearly dropped the entire tray. Trillian. That's what she called him. Trillian."

Driskoll looked at Kellach, but his brother was lost in thought about something else and didn't seem to register the name.

It didn't seem like the kind of place Trillian would choose for his socializing. He was much more likely to be spotted at Moors Point or the Grinning Hippogriff, places where he could boast about his brave work for the watch and have travelers and merchants, presumably impressed by his tales of daring, offer to buy him a drink or a bite to eat.

Patrons of the Skinned Cat in Broken Town didn't exactly have a lot of extra money to be buying watchers a pint of ale. And helping himself to other people's food didn't seem at all like Trillian, even when he was in one of his uppity moods. Their father made sure that all his watchers behaved courteously, especially when in uniform.

Driskoll was still thinking about Trillian and trying to imagine the scene at the pub when he realized Royma was still talking.

"And as if that's not bad enough, now all the watch commanders are helping themselves to things in shops and even inside people's homes!" she said. "Over in the Phoenix Quarter early in the afternoon, the watch was blaming the people of Broken Town for the robberies. Of course, none of us here believed that for a minute. And how could anyone else believe it either? The watchers have been stealing things in full uniform and in full view of everyone! I always knew those watchers were crooks." Royma snorted. "They claim to be keeping this town safe, but if you ask me, they're the ones who need watching."

"That's ridiculous," Driskoll said. "My dad would never tolerate something like that." Driskoll asked.

Royma's left eye twitched a bit, as if riled by the mention of the captain of the watch. "I'm sorry to have to be the one to tell you boys this, but your father isn't in charge anymore."

Kellach seemed to come to attention at that. "What do you mean?"

"It seems he's in prison," Moyra's mother went on. "It might be best if you two stay here for awhile. In the meantime, you'd better get cleaned up. There is a most unusual smell about you—all three of you." Royma waved her hand in front of her nose. "Now I need to get back to the market. I left Carrie Hurtle watching over my stand while I came back here to check on Breddo. But you know how she is. She couldn't sell a doorknob to save her life."

And with that, Royma slipped out the back door.

CHAPTER

22

"D ad's . . . in jail? I can't believe it." Driskoll shook his
head. "Most of those prisoners hate him. He won't last
the night."

Kellach dropped his pack and placed it on the small kitchen
table. "This just means we have to hurry."

"Let's get the attavus's eye cleaned up," Driskoll said as he
pulled the drawstring pouch containing the eye out of Kellach's
pack.

"You touch it first," Moyra said.

"Not so tough, are you?" Driskoll teased. He held his breath
as he slid the eyeball and surrounding tissue out of the pouch.
"Let's just boil it, shall we?"

"No!" cried Kellach. But it was too late. Driskoll dropped the
mass into the boiling pot of water before anyone could stop him.
"Quick, Moyra, where's your ladle?" She grabbed it from the
counter and swiftly scooped the eyeball out of the cast-iron pot.

Only there wasn't an eyeball left in the water. The ladle now held a small, gleaming stone. Moyra put it on the kitchen table and then wiped it dry with a kitchen cloth. The stone was like quartz crystal, only it had an iridescent blue glow coming from inside it.

"Amazing," Kellach whispered in awe.

"Is it the seeing gem?" Driskoll asked excitedly.

"I think it is," Kellach said, still in a state of disbelief. "If I'm right, all I have to do is hold it in my hand and look someone directly in the eye." Kellach gripped the crystal in his palm and stared at Driskoll for several long moments. A frown spread across his face. "It doesn't work!"

Driskoll grabbed the gem from his brother. "Let me try." He looked at Moyra, and slowly she seemed to change before his eyes. He saw a graceful, beautiful young woman. She looked successful—and happy, as if she finally didn't have to worry every day about her parents and whether there'd be food for them to eat. He looked at Kellach and saw a wizard more powerful and cunning than Zendric.

"Gods," he breathed. "It does work! It's almost like looking into the future, but it's not the future. It's as if I can see you as you really are, as you're meant to be."

Kellach snorted. "That's your imagination, Dris. The seeing gem works only for someone who has powerful magic, a wizard like Zendric or Griffin—or me."

"But I saw . . . " Driskoll started to say.

"You imagined," Kellach corrected. "You have a great gift of imagination, Dris, I'll give you that. But that doesn't mean you'll be able to see the Trickster through its disguises."

Driskoll didn't say anything. He spun the blue gem on the table.

"Now what are we going to do?" Moyra asked. "That gem could have saved your father. It's hopeless now."

"*We* can still save our father," Kellach said.

"Let's hope you can," came a voice from the back doorway.

CHAPTER

23

It was Trillian.

"How did you know where to find us?" Driskoll asked. "Is Dad looking for us?" It just figured that Trillian would show up now.

"Hey, Driskoll," Trillian said. "Your father didn't send me. I was just worried about you three. Are you all right?"

Trillian worried about them? Never even for a minute had Trillian seemed genuinely concerned with Driskoll or Kellach, or anyone else who couldn't help him advance in his career. Still, Trillian's words were kind.

"I'm sorry to be the bearer of bad news," Trillian began. That's odd too, Driskoll thought. Trillian usually gloated when there was bad news to tell, especially when it involved Driskoll, Kellach, or Moyra.

"We know the news," Kellach said irritably. "We just heard that Dad's in jail."

"Who put him there?" Driskoll asked. "Who arrested him?"

"I did," Trillian said, his head hung low. Now he looked genuinely depressed.

Just then, a flash of silver swooped into the room, skimming past Trillian's right ear. Trillian's hand flew to his head. "Ow! What in the gods' names was that?"

The sound of wings flapping registered in Driskoll's ears just as he saw a tiny dragon landing on Kellach's shoulder.

"Locky!" Kellach cried. "What are you doing here? Weren't you locked in the closet? How did you get out?"

The dragonet started trilling and chirping and tugging at Kellach's robes. Kellach leaned in to listen closely.

At last Kellach looked up. "He says Dad let him out of the closet just before the watch took him away. Locky says Dad told him to come find me and tell us what had happened. He wants us to meet him at the jail."

Kellach petted Locky's shiny head. "I can't believe you found us, boy. You're so smart."

Locky twisted his head away from Kellach and took off again. He swooped across the room and landed on the table, grabbing the seeing gem between his small paws.

"Locky! Put that away," Kellach scolded him. Locky chirped. He dropped the gem in the drawstring pouch and lifted it off the table.

Trillian's eyes flashed as he took in the dragonet and the rock he now carried.

"We have to get to Watchers' Hall," Driskoll said. "Dad needs us."

"No!" Trillian shouted. "I mean," he added, lowering his voice, "you three should stay right here in this cozy home. Your father wouldn't want you to see him in jail."

Kellach gave the recruit a weird look. "No, Driskoll's right. Dad said he needed us." Kellach grabbed his pack off the table. "Are you coming, Moyra?"

"Of course!" Moyra was already heading out the door.

Trillian looked at the dragonet, his eyes narrowing. And then his expression softened. "If you'll allow me, I'd be happy to accompany you. The streets of Curston aren't safe at this hour."

Kellach shrugged. "Whatever you say, Trillian." And then he slipped out the door.

■　■　■　■　■

As the four kids walked through the street toward watch headquarters, Trillian kept glancing back at Locky. And then at Driskoll.

"Kellach, why don't you lead us for awhile?" Trillian said. "I'll bring up the rear. That way I can watch you—do my job as a watcher, and make sure you're safe." He laughed.

"I am really concerned about your father, you know," Trillian said, as he walked alongside Driskoll.

"Right," Driskoll said. "You're only ever concerned for yourself, Trillian."

"Locky! What are you doing?" Kellach cried as the dragonet leaped off his shoulder and into Driskoll's arms.

"It's okay, Kell. I've got him," Driskoll said. It was odd for Locky to choose to hitchhike a ride on Driskoll. The dragonet was quite attached to his own master, Kellach. Driskoll noticed Trillian looking curiously at Locky—and then intently at the bag the dragon clutched.

"What do you have there, little guy?" Trillian purred in a sickly sweet voice. Trillian lunged for the magical creature.

Locky began a high-pitched chirping that almost sounded like shrieking. His long neck jutted out and nipped Trillian on the ear.

"Ow! I'm going to wring that little monster's neck!" Trillian growled. He reached out and tried to grab Locky by the throat. But Locky flew just beyond his reach.

"Keep your hands off my dragon!" Kellach cried, taking a swing at Trillian.

"Driskoll, help me!"

Driskoll kicked Trillian in the shin and then rammed his head into Trillian's stomach. Moyra jumped up on the young recruit's back, pulling his hair.

"Get off me, you ruffian!" Trillian whirled around, tossing Moyra to the cobblestones. "You and your worthless friends can find your own way to Watchers' Hall! Hellhounds can eat you alive for all I care." The young recruit began marching down the street.

Locky kept up a constant chirping, trying to burrow himself back in Kellach's robes. "Ow! Locky! Stop it." Kellach said. Locky lost his grip on the small drawstring pouch. As it fell, the seeing gem slipped out.

Driskoll grabbed the gem before it hit the ground. He fingered it quickly, just for a few seconds. But those few seconds were enough.

As Trillian reached the end of the street, he looked back over his shoulder, locking eyes with Driskoll. And instead of the healthy young recruit, Driskoll saw sickly gray skin, gangly arms, and green slitted eyes.

Driskoll was staring directly at the Trickster.

CHAPTER

24

"That was weird," Moyra said as she got to her feet. "Trillian may be a self-centered jerk, but I've never seen him so . . . violent."

"That wasn't Trillian," Driskoll said, slipping the gem back into its pouch. "We've just met the Trickster."

"What?" Moyra and Kellach said at the same time.

"Listen, Kell, I know you don't think I'm magical enough to see with the seeing gem," Driskoll was talking extremely fast, wanting to get it all out before anyone stopped him. "But for just a few seconds. I had my hands on the stone, and I saw the Trickster. It wasn't Trillian at all. It stared back at me—and then it disappeared."

Neither Kellach nor Moyra said anything.

"You don't believe me, do you?"

"Was it . . . was it like Griffin described it?" Kellach asked.

"I don't remember every detail about what you said Griffin

saw, but one moment I was looking at Trillian, and the next I saw this gangly, skinny creature with gray skin. It turned and looked at me with its green eyes. That's all I remember about the face. The eyes."

"You could have taken that description straight from Griffin's book," Moyra said.

"But I didn't!" Driskoll said. "I know what I saw when I was holding that gem."

"You could be right," Kellach said.

Driskoll felt too frightened about what they might find ahead at the prison to argue anymore. "Kell, Moyra, it doesn't matter what you think. Let's just keep moving. We need to hurry. We need to see Dad and tell him about the Trickster."

"You are right about that, little brother." Kellach said, and the three Knights took off, hurrying through Broken Town and onto watch headquarters.

When they reached Watchers' Hall, they rushed through the tower entrance and into the prison office beyond.

Driskoll expected to see their old friend, Guffy, waiting behind the duty desk, as usual.

But instead of Guffy's familiar face, Driskoll saw Trillian.

The hairs on the back of Driskoll's neck stood up. He pulled out the stone and gripped it in his palm.

Kellach began walking slowly toward the young recruit. "I won't have you attacking my dragon again. I could have you jailed for that."

Trillian's jaw gaped. "I don't know what you're talking about," Trillain said as he rose from his chair.

"You know very well what I'm talking about. You just met us at Moyra's house—"

Trillian cut him off. "No, I've been here all afternoon. Guffy has the day off."

Driskoll stepped in front of his brother. "Look, Trillian. Just ignore him. It's too much to explain, but we need to see our father. Can you bring him up here? It's very important."

"I don't know . . . It's against regulations to allow visitations at this hour. And especially in the prison office!"

"Please Trillian," Driskoll pleaded, "it's a matter of life or death."

Trillian stood up and opened the ironbound door behind him. "Fine. But I'm only doing this because I feel sorry for you two. It's enough that your poor mother had to go and—"

"Just go!" Driskoll barked. He surprised himself by the force in his voice. He sounded almost exactly like his father.

Trillian must have thought the same thing because he snapped to attention. "I'll be right back." He slipped into the dark staircase that led down to the prison below.

Kellach stared at Driskoll, his jaw gaping. "Wow, that was impressive."

"Weren't you worried *that* was the Trickster?" Moyra teased.

Driskoll held up the stone before tucking it back into his

jacket pocket. "I used the stone. I could tell *that* was the real Trillian."

Kellach eyed his brother strangely but as he was about to speak, the ironbound door behind the prison desk opened. In the doorway, stood Trillian. But he was alone.

"Where's my father?" Kellach demanded.

Just then, two more figures appeared in the doorway. One was Torin. The captain's wrists were bound in iron circlets.

"Dad!" Kellach shouted.

A young recruit held fast to Torin's forearms. "Let go of me, Trillian," Torin shouted. The young man relaxed his grip, and stepping back, bumped into the other Trillian.

"Who are you?" the first Trillian said.

"Who are you?" said the other Trillian.

"Dad!" Driskoll shouted. "One of these Trillians is an imposter. But I can tell the right one." Driskoll rushed through the door and into the passageway. He stumbled as he came to a halt in front of his father.

The pouch containing the gem flew out of his pocket, skidding across the stone floor and disappearing in the dark corridor.

"No!" Driskoll cried.

"What was that?" both Trillians said at once.

Driskoll scrambled to his feet and plowed past one Trillian, intent on retrieving the gem.

The other Trillian grabbed him. "Stay here," Trillian said.

I should be able to figure this out, Driskoll thought. Which-ever Trillian is the most annoying and smarmy, must be the Trillian who is authentic.

"Take your hands off him," the other Trillian said.

Ha! That must be the Trickster, Driskoll thought. The real Trillian wouldn't try to protect him like that.

"Don't tell me what to do," said the other Trillian. "My job is to protect the citizens of Curston, and that includes the captain's son. If you were the real me, you'd do the same. These boys know that I will protect them."

Or is that the Trickster? Driskoll thought. If only he had the gem.

"I'll get to the bottom of this," Torin said. "I am still your captain."

"Be quiet!" both Trillians said at once. They glared at each other.

"You're no longer the captain," said Trillian.

"You're a prisoner, Torin, so keep quiet," said the other Trillian.

Driskoll, Kellach, and Moyra watched with fascination, their heads turning from one Trillian to the other, trying to make sense of it all.

"Let me have the prisoner," said one Trillian.

"He's my prisoner," said the other.

"Sir," one Trillian addressed Torin. "You have my assurance that no harm will come to your sons if you cooperate. I've been friends with Kell and Dris far too long to let any evil power harm them."

Aha! Driskoll thought. Trillian never called him his nickname. That one must be the Trickster.

Driskoll lunged at the Trickster-Trillian. Before Driskoll could reach him, Trillian stepped back, pushing Torin down the steep stone stairs.

"Dad!" Driskoll called. His eyes narrowed, and he bent down and ran full force with his head ramming into Trillian's stomach.

He banged Trillian up against the stone wall with a force so hard that it reverberated through Driskoll's head and down his spine. He'd never known pain like this, but it was too late to slow down now.

He head-butted Trillian again and again, until he felt arms tugging him away.

Driskoll swung his right fist blindly at the attacker from behind. "Dris, it's me!" Kellach said. "This might be the true Trillian."

"I don't think so," Driskoll muttered, panting.

A son's got to do what a son's got to do, he thought. And with that Driskoll took his left foot and planted it firmly on Kellach's groin, pushing him away.

"Has the Trickster taken you over too?" Kellach gasped.

Driskoll had no time to answer, nor any extra energy to try to explain.

One Trillian was still on the ground, grasping his knee and trying to get up. Blood dripped from a cut above his left eye.

The Trickster version of Trillian was trying to rise up from the ground. The drawstring pouch rested by his left leg. Driskoll's eyes went wide.

He swooped down, pouncing as much of his weight and energy as he could on the Trickster-Trillian. Just as he landed on the being, it became nearly half its Trillian size. Then, the clothes disappeared. Driskoll leaned over and wrapped his hand around the small pouch, fingering the stone inside.

Suddenly, Driskoll looked down again and found himself on top of a clammy gray being.

The Trickster turned in Driskoll's grasp and bore its green eyes into him. Driskoll felt something tighten around his neck. He tried to pry the Trickster's long, strong fingers from their vice-like grasp around his neck.

This is what it's like to be choked to death, thought Driskoll. He coughed once, twice. Then there was no air left to cough.

Driskoll's body went completely limp.

25

D ris, Dris, are you okay?" Kell was kneeling at his brother's side.

"What happened?" Driskoll muttered.

"Trillian, I mean the Trickster, almost choked you to death. But just as you blacked out, he disappeared."

Moyra came running up the stairs.

"Your father is three flights down. Something might be broken," she said. "I can't move him."

Trillian—the true Trillian—groaned from the dark side of the corridor. "Torin's seen tougher days. He will be all right. Go after that imposter! Go!"

Driskoll sat up and took some welcome breaths.

"I'm okay," he said. "He's right. We've got to go." He sprang to his feet and held up the pouch with the seeing gem. "Look. I've got the gem. We'll be able to find the Trickster now."

"But what about Dad?" Kellach asked.

"He said he'd be okay. To do what we had to do," Moyra said. "But what about him?" Moyra cocked her head back at Trillian. "You sure that's the true Trillian?"

Driskoll fingered the gem and nodded.

"I'm the true Trillian," growled Trillian. "I told you—go! I'll get word to the other watchers. But you three need to track that imposter, whoever it was."

"The Trickster," Kellach and Driskoll said at once.

Locky chirped excitedly.

"I'm with him," Moyra said. "Let's get going."

∎ ▮ ∎ ▮ ∎

Tracking a Trickster wouldn't be exactly easy. By the time the trio got outside Watchers' Hall, they had no idea which way the Trickster might have gone, and no clue what it would look like now. Had it gone back to being Trillian? Would it dare to be Torin again? Or maybe it had returned to Broken Town in the form of Breddo, Moyra's father. Driskoll and Moyra looked at Kellach, hoping he might have a logical plan of attack.

"We know the Trickster was hired by someone in Curston to discredit Dad," Kellach said. "It seems logical then that it would go to where the most people are: the market at Main Square."

"Or maybe to the Phoenix Quarter," Driskoll added.

"Stop talking, you two, and get moving!" Moyra said. "Follow me. I know a shortcut through Broken Town. Let's cut through there to get to the market."

It was a good thing that both Kellach and Driskoll were quick runners, because keeping up with Moyra was serious business.

When they got to Main Square, Moyra pulled them to a stop. The market was settling down for the day, with farmers and hawkers packing up their wares.

"We'll need to split up to survey the area and see if we can find the Trickster," Kellach said. "I'll take Locky and you take the gem, Dris."

Driskoll looked at his brother, shocked. Did Kellach believe the gem worked for him now?

"And I'll take the rooftops," Moyra said.

"Thought you'd say that," Kellach said. "Let's head south through the square and then into the Phoenix Quarter."

Kellach was just finishing his sentence when loud voices erupted a few market stalls away.

"You can't take that from me without paying!" said a gravelly voiced woman.

"I am the captain of the watch, and I am in charge of everything that happens in Curston," said a voice that sounded like Torin's. "It is a matter of great urgency that I take this fine blade of yours. You'll thank me later."

"Thank you later? Why, I'll thank you now."

Driskoll, Kellach, and Moyra got there just in time to see a tall hunched woman jump on Torin's back. Driskoll didn't even need to touch the seeing gem to know with certainty that they were just six feet from the Trickster.

The woman probably weighed close to two hundred pounds, and the Trickster staggered under her weight.

"Let go of me, you old bitty!" The Trickster began turning in circles, flinging the old woman around. It finally pried her hands away from its shoulders, and with one forceful shove it pushed her down to the ground, knocking over a table of her knives for sale.

"Oh, you're insisting I take more, are you? Well, thank you for supporting the watch," said the Trickster. It swept another knife off the ground and took off at a run.

All of a sudden, Driskoll had an idea.

"Dad! Wait for me!" he called.

Kellach and Moyra stared at him in disbelief.

"I'm acting," Driskoll whispered to them. "Just watch!"

"Dad!" Driskoll called again, as he jogged after the Trickster. "I need your help. Please wait for me."

The Trickster looked back as it ran. People in the market surely recognized the face of Torin, and to hear a son calling for his father and to see the father keep running away would seem suspicious even to the ignorant.

The Trickster stopped and paused, as if waiting for Driskoll, and then it broke into a run again.

"Dad! I said wait up!" Driskoll called in his best impression of a whiny five-year-old. He was actually enjoying himself and this little game. Moyra ran beside him.

"I'm going up," she said.

Driskoll nodded. He didn't know where Kellach had gone. He was keeping his eyes on the Trickster-turned-Torin.

A man near a potato cart stuck out his leg. The Trickster stumbled over the sudden obstacle and fell flat on its face.

"What's with you, you beast!" the potato man said. "Can't you see your boy is calling you?"

The Trickster stood quickly, pulling one of its knives out. "Don't you ever try that again," it said, with the point of the blade under the man's chin.

Driskoll came to a sudden halt. He didn't want the Trickster to make any quick moves that might draw blood. The Trickster looked directly at Driskoll.

"Dad?" Driskoll said in a whiny, shaky voice. This time, he didn't have to act to make his voice to shake.

As Driskoll stared at the Trickster, the face of Torin stared back, but the eyes began to turn green.

The Trickster turned its back to Driskoll, tickled the potato man's face with the sharp point of its knife, and laughed.

The creature took a few brisk steps away and its appearance changed effortlessly. Driskoll didn't even realize what was happening until he saw a young laundress with a long brown braid down her back and a basket full of dirty clothes in her arms.

"Stop her!" Driskoll called, pointing at the Trickster-turned-laundress. The Trickster flung the basket of dirty clothes back over its head and kept running.

Driskoll peeled a stinky shirt from his face and tossed it off to the side. He briefly wondered how in the world the Trickster managed to get such truly filthy garments.

The laundry basket tumbled a few feet down the road. Driskoll kicked it to one side and broke into an all-out run. He snaked through the market stalls, out of Main Square, and onto the street that led through the heart of the Phoenix Quarter.

"Stop her! She stole my grandma's knives!" he called out. He suspected it was pointless to ask passersby to stop a girl being chased by a young boy who, considering his appearance, looked like a ruffian. But it was the best idea he had.

"Stop her! She stole my grandma's knives!" Driskoll heard his own voice say. Only he wasn't talking.

In an instant, the Trickster had changed from a laundress into . . . Driskoll! The Trickster-turned-Driskoll was running at an easy pace and pointing up to the rooftops above.

"Stop her!" Trickster-Driskoll cried. "That's Moyra the thief girl, and she stole from my grandma!"

Driskoll saw that Moyra really was up above, leaping in her effortless way from one rooftop to another. Surely she would know that it was the Trickster calling about her. Then again, hadn't the real Driskoll just called out "Stop her"?

Driskoll had never felt as strange as he did now, running and huffing and puffing and sweating. Running after himself! Could things get any stranger?

Kellach popped out of an alleyway.

"Driskoll!" Kellach called.

Driskoll tried to wave to get his brother's attention, but the Trickster version of Driskoll got to Kellach first.

"Hey brother, take this!" and the Trickster used a right-legged sidekick to slam into Kellach's stomach and knock him down flat.

"What in the—" Kellach cried. Locky chirped nonstop. The Trickster kept running, and the real Driskoll caught up to his brother.

"It wasn't me!" Driskoll said, bending down by Kellach.

"Who are you?" Kellach asked, his eyes narrowing. "How do I know you're my brother?"

"Griffin!" Driskoll said.

Kellach looked at his brother blankly for a minute, and then he remembered their code word. A smile tugged at the corners of his mouth.

"Yeah, Griffin." He brushed off his robes and stood up.

"I have to get running again," Driskoll said.

"I'll head west a little and try to cut it off," Kellach said, and he raced back down the alley.

Driskoll nodded and raced off. He hurtled down the street, turned the corner, and kept on running. But it was no use. He had lost sight of the Trickster, which was weird because that meant he'd lost sight of himself.

He stopped and looked up above for Moyra, but didn't see any sign of her or her swift shadow up on the roofs.

"Dris! Over here!" he heard Kellach's voice. He looked around and saw Kellach down on the ground outside an abandoned shop, its windows barred with boards.

"I'm hurt, and the Trickster took Locky!"

Driskoll hurried over to his brother.

"And now I'm taking you," Kellach grabbed Driskoll and pulled him inside the shop.

CHAPTER

26

Moyra sat inside the shop, ropes binding her arms to the back of a sturdy bench. She had a rag tied around her mouth to keep her quiet, but it didn't seem to be of much use. Driskoll could hear a string of muffled curses coming from beneath the dirty rag.

"Maybe you should have kept a finger on the pulse of that seeing gem all afternoon, my good lad." The voice sounded like Kellach's, but the words were nothing like the way Kellach spoke. Driskoll wanted to kick himself for being so stupid. Standing before him was the Trickster.

"Where's my brother?" Driskoll demanded.

"A fact I'd be eager to know myself." The Trickster pushed Driskoll onto the bench next to Moyra and began tying his arms. "As soon as I'm done with you, I'll be going out to lure him back here too."

For a brief moment, the Trickster morphed into Driskoll's

shape and called out in his voice. "Kellach! Help me!" The Trickster laughed, the noise like rocks shaking through its throat. "If I'd known what a pest you would be, I would have eliminated you when I first set eyes on you. Remember? Yesterday morning, in the market?"

The Trickster changed again, this time into the half-orc that had terrorized Driskoll only yesterday. "Your expression was priceless." The Trickster laughed again.

Driskoll gasped. "That was you?"

"Of course, you little fool. I was running away from setting the fire at the wainwright's." The Trickster's orc hands clenched into fists, and it leaned forward until its red pimpled nose nearly brushed Driskoll's own."Your little stunt slowed me down severely. But it didn't stop me." The Trickster stepped back, sneering. "No, nothing will stop me now. Your father's already in prison, and the watch is in shambles. Everything is going exactly according to our plan."

"*Our* plan?" Driskoll asked. "Who sent you here? Who hired you?"

"That's of no consequence to you." The Trickster pulled a knife out of the half-orc's purple robes.

"It doesn't matter what you do to me, but please don't hurt Moyra or Kellach," Driskoll said.

Moyra glared at the Trickster, tugging hard against the ropes holding her arms back. Her angry cries were muffled beneath her gag.

"Such a brave lad for a little brother and the son of that scum Torin," the Trickster said, sharpening the knife on a piece of stainless steel. "Now, I'm enjoying our little conversation here, but I think I'll need to gag you too."

With a flick of its knife, the Trickster cut a swath of fabric from its robes, then wrapped it around Driskoll's mouth. Driskoll tried to scream, but it was no use.

The Trickster stood back to admire its work. "Now, this is fun, isn't it?"

"I think the fun is over," a voice thundered.

Driskoll's eyes flew to the doorway. There stood Torin. The real Kellach was right behind him, with Locky clutching his shoulder.

In a flash, the Trickster changed into a six-foot-five-inch muscle-bound man, complete with protective armor and a sword in his right hand.

It leaped into position, pointing the sword at both Kellach and Torin.

Torin pulled his own sword out, and the Trickster made another sword appear in its left hand. The Trickster lunged at both of them. With one swift and gentle move, the point of Torin's sword met the Trickster's with a loud clank. Kellach ducked.

The older boy raced to his brother and Moyra. He pulled a dagger off his belt and cut through Driskoll's ropes.

Kellach moved to the right and did the same for Moyra, cutting cleanly through her ropes while Driskoll wrenched the

gag off his mouth. Driskoll leaned over and helped Moyra untie the rag from her mouth. Moyra was still shouting.

"—And if Torin doesn't cut you to pieces, I will—" With a start, she realized the gag was gone. She looked at Driskoll and Kellach. "Thanks." Her voice was hoarse.

Driskoll motioned for his brother to come closer.

"Listen," he whispered. "I have an idea. If we all three touch the seeing gem at once and look directly at the Trickster, maybe we can turn it into its true essence." He took the drawstring bag from his jacket pocket and shook out the gem.

Torin, an expert swordsman, was keeping the Trickster at bay, even though Torin had a splint on his left leg and appeared to be in a great deal of pain.

Driskoll realized that they certainly didn't need the seeing gem now to know whether Torin was the true Torin or the Trickster-as-Torin. Only the true Torin could fight through such intense pain.

Driskoll held out the seeing gem, and Moyra and Kellach each put two of their fingers on it. Locky climbed down Kellach's arm and put a paw on the seeing gem too.

Immediately the tall armored fighter showed its true form. The skinny, gray, hairless being with green eyes was standing before them, still with a sword in each hand. It sensed that its form had changed to the three of them.

"Gods, Driskoll!" Kellach breathed. "So that's what the Trickster looks like."

The creature turned its noseless head toward them and looked at them with its slitted eyes.

"Who sent you?" Driskoll demanded.

The Trickster shook its head, savoring its secret. Without looking back, it blocked a low slash from Torin's sword. Then it turned and redoubled its efforts, backing the captain into a corner.

"Stay back, children!" Torin called. "This muscleman is no match for you three."

"It didn't work!" Moyra whispered through clenched teeth. "We can see the Trickster, but your dad can't. He doesn't see the Trickster's true essence."

"I have another idea," Driskoll said quietly. "Don't let your fingers off the gem. Follow me."

Carefully the trio moved in step with Driskoll toward the Trickster. "With your other hand, touch the Trickster. Keep your fingers on the gem, but we all need to all touch it at once. Locky, you help, too." No one questioned him.

Locky leaped off Kellach's arm and ran under the Trickster's feet. The creature tripped.

"I've got you now!" Torin stood over the Trickster, his sword pointed directly at its chest.

"Dad, you can't kill it," Driskoll said. "Don't try. It won't work yet." He reached out his hand toward the Trickster's body. "Wait, just a second."

And it took only a second. All three of them put a hand

somewhere on the Trickster's disgusting gray skin. Driskoll could see Moyra wince as she touched it.

The power of the seeing gem and the three Knights together turned the Trickster into its true essence. Driskoll's hunch was right. Now even Torin could see the creature's true form.

Torin stepped back in surprise, perhaps even disgust.

"Now, Dad! Now!" Driskoll cried.

"I think I'll arrest it instead," Torin said. "I'll take it into the possession of the watch. We need to know who hired it. We need to know where it came from."

The Trickster turned its glowing green eyes toward Driskoll. For once, Driskoll knew exactly what to do. He saw no need for stories. No need for words. He tore the sword out of his father's hand, and with both of his hands he gripped on the handle. He raised it high above his head, and with all of his body weight, he forced the sword down into the chest of the Trickster.

CHAPTER

27

Now that a day had passed since he'd killed the Trickster, Driskoll wished he'd held out for the Trickster's story.

Driskoll sat at the kitchen table, staring down at his half-eaten dinner. Around him, family and friends were feasting on a celebratory meal of roasted pork, potatoes, beef tartar, eggplant, kale, and sweet potatoes.

They'd invited Trillian, Kalmbur, the merchant guildmasters Mormo and Farley, and Moyra, of course. Torin was so grateful for his freedom that he had even insisted that Moyra bring her parents too. Breddo and Royma were shocked by the invitation, but they were not ones to turn down the chance to join in such a sumptuous feast.

Driskoll noticed that the adults got along better and better, the more cider they passed around. It was nice to see Royma looking relaxed and happy. It was even nicer to see Breddo enjoying a good meal and talking with watchers as if they were friends rather than enemies.

Driskoll sighed. He wished he felt more like celebrating. But something tugged at his conscience.

If only he had been able to find out who had hired the Trickster. That was his one regret. Of course, the stories he could make up about the Trickster's motives might be just as good. Still, Driskoll longed for some authenticity in his writing. He imagined it would be a little difficult to always have himself as the hero of the tale of the Trickster of Curston.

Driskoll smiled. Then again, he was the hero, wasn't he?

From what Kellach had told them about Griffin's interview with the Trickster more than forty years ago, Driskoll had determined that it would be pointless to try to kill the monster unless it was in its true form. It was a wild hunch that if the Knights of the Silver Dragon combined their power by touching the seeing gem and the Trickster, they might force the shapeshifter into its true essence.

He knew the Trickster would need to be put to its death right away. Capture would be pointless. It would be too easy for a creature such as the Trickster to escape. There was good reason, Driskoll thought, that the shapeshifter had been called the Trickster for so many generations. It was an elusive, stealthy, and, of course, tricky creature.

Kellach stood up and clinked a glass of milk with a spoon, shaking Driskoll from his reverie.

"This dinner is for you, Dris," Kellach said. "If it weren't for you, we would never have destroyed the Trickster."

"Thanks, Kell," Driskoll said. "I wasn't so sure you believed in me."

"I didn't believe in you," Kellach said flatly. Then he uttered three words that Driskoll rarely heard pass his brother's lips. "I was wrong."

He raised his glass of milk. "To Driskoll!"

"To Driskoll!" the group around the table repeated, and they drained their glasses.

The others went back to talking and eating. But Driskoll had eaten his fill. He picked up the seeing gem and rubbed it gently. Sometimes he couldn't stop himself from sneaking a peek at Moyra or Kellach when he touched the stone.

Now he fingered it absentmindedly and looked around the table, pausing at Moyra, Kellach, Trillian, and Torin in turn.

Just for curiosity, he looked at the other adults at the table too. With the seeing gem, Kalmbur looked much the same as he did in person, except his true goodness radiated out of him like a bright white light. The gem showed a vision of the successful artist Royma might have been if her troubled life hadn't held her back. Even Breddo's true essence proved what Driskoll had always known. In spite of his hijinks, at heart, Breddo was a good man.

But when Driskoll came to Mormo, he stopped. Mormo's true essence looked twisted and old, all hunched into himself, as if he didn't trust anyone around him.

When Driskoll looked from left to right, from Mormo to Torin, there was a black mist blocking the two essences. When he looked from right to left, from Torin to Mormo, there was no blockage.

He dropped the stone and took a big gulp of milk.

Driskoll picked up the seeing gem again and started looking around the table at each guest, watching the progression as he moved from one to another. Nothing was in the way. People were open, relaxed, and happy.

Until he got to Mormo. Again, when his eyes moved from Mormo to Torin, a black haze seemed to block the way.

Suddenly Driskoll understood.

"It was you!" Driskoll yelled, standing up and knocking his chair behind him.

His voice managed to interrupt all three conversations that were going on.

"Driskoll, what is this rude outburst during our celebratory dinner?" Torin asked sternly.

"It was you," Driskoll said pointing at Mormo. "It was the guildmaster. He's the one who hired the Trickster in the first place. He wants you out!"

Torin turned to his guests. "My deepest apologies, friends." The captain looked at his son, his brow wrinkled. "Driskoll, please sit down."

"No, I won't sit down." Driskoll stamped his foot. "He failed this time with the Trickster, but who knows? He may have something else planned, if he has enough money."

"Driskoll, please! Let's discuss this after—" Torin began.

"Let the boy speak, Torin," Mormo said, waving for Torin to calm down. "I'd love to hear what evidence young Driskoll has that leads him to accuse me of such treachery."

Driskoll pinched the gem between his forefinger and his thumb and held it up for everyone at the table to see. The candlelight glinted off the bluish stone.

Royma gasped. "That must be worth a fortune."

"This is a seeing gem." Driskoll said. "It's how I was able to identify the Trickster. It shows the true essence of a person." Driskoll glared at Mormo. "Your true essence is black!"

"Black?" Mormo said calmly, a confident smile on his face. "And what does that prove? I'm sure everything looks black when viewed through a lump of stone."

Torin looked from Mormo to his son, clearly puzzled. "Is that all you have to say, Driskoll?"

Driskoll looked to his brother for help, but Kellach lifted his shoulders. Moyra shook her head.

"It's true!" Driskoll insisted. "Why won't anyone believe me?"

The table was silent.

"Well, now that's settled," Mormo said, taking another bite of beef. He wiped his mouth with his napkin and looked back at Driskoll. "I must admit that is a pretty bauble you've found there, boy. You wouldn't want it to be stolen. Why don't you let me keep it at my shop? Here give it to me." He reached out to snatch the stone from Driskoll's hand, but Driskoll pulled back reflexively.

"No!"

"May I give it a try?" They all turned to the new voice that had entered the room.

Zendric stood there, in the doorway, wrapped in his wizard robes. "I got your note, Kellach." Zendric held up a gnarled wooden pencil and smiled.

"You made it!" Kellach jumped up and offered his chair to Zendric. "I invited Zendric to have dessert with us if he got back in time," Kellach explained to the others as Zendric took Kellach's place at the table.

Driskoll passed the seeing gem to the wizard.

"Ah, a lovely gem indeed," Zendric murmured. "It's small, but powerful if used in the right hands." Zendric looked Driskoll in the eye. "I understand that you have the right hands, my friend."

Driskoll beamed.

"I see it has not led you astray yet," Zendric added. "Not even tonight." Zendric gripped the stone in his hands. "Such an interesting array of guests, here tonight, Torin." Zendric looked at each person in turn. When he came to Mormo, he stopped.

Mormo started twitching in his chair, shifting his weight back and forth from side to side.

"An interesting array, indeed." Zendric handed the stone back to Driskoll and walked over to stand behind Mormo's chair.

"I think the guildmaster may be able to give you some background on the Trickster, Torin," Zendric said. He rested his hand on the shoulder of the other merchant, sitting next to Mormo. "His colleague here, Miss Farley, seems to know a bit about the whole arrangement as well."

The other guildmaster turned bright red in the face. She stood, holding her hands up defensively. "All right! I can't take this any more. Mormo made me do it . . . I didn't want anything to do with this, but . . . "

"Mormo . . . Mormo?" Breddo snapped his fingers and pointed at the guildmaster. "I knew I recognized that name! You're the evil merchant that used to cheat the people of Broken Town! You were the merchant who was robbed by Maria and M—"

Royma poked Breddo in the ribs. "Ah-hem. I mean who was robbed." He glared at Mormo accusingly. "How did a crook like you ever become merchant guildmaster?"

"Bribery, how else?" Farley answered for Mormo. "But I'm done with your bribes, Mormo. No amount of money is going to keep me from speaking the truth. This has gone far enough. I'm going to tell them everything."

Mormo sneered. "All right. It was me. I hired the Trickster." Mormo glared at Torin. "I was sick and tired of you and your imbecilic watch after that ridiculous theft. You call yourself captain of the watch? You're practically in league with the thieves. Those two sisters stole my gold! And you knew it. But you didn't do a thing to punish them. Then I found out you had personally called off the investigation. That was when I knew. I didn't want revenge on those girls. I wanted revenge on you . . . "

"Is that what this was all about?" Torin shook his head. "We had no evidence to go on, Mormo. You refused to cooperate with the investigation. I had heard rumors about you cheating the poor folk of Broken Town, but until then, I wasn't prepared to believe it. To be perfectly frank, if I had had more evidence, *you* would be in prison right now. Cheating innocent poor people is not only a crime, it's downright despicable."

"Innocent?" Mormo scoffed. "Those fools deserve everything they get. Their problems are sucking this city dry. I was doing Curston a service, I tell you."

Torin's eyes narrowed and he stood up. "That will be quite enough, Mormo. Trillian, Kalmbur, and I will escort you to Watchers' Hall before you say anything more to incriminate yourself. You too, Farley."

Trillian and Kalmbur marched the two guildmasters away from the dinner table. Torin held the door open.

Driskoll waved. "Please, no need to apologize for leaving early," he called as the three watchers escorted Mormo and Farley out the door.

Royma and Breddo both watched, their jaws gaping.

After a moment, Royma turned to Kellach. "I had no idea your father cared so much for the people of Broken Town. That was positively . . . "

"Gallant?" Moyra suggested, wrapping her arm around Driskoll's shoulder.

Zendric took Torin's seat at the head of the table. "You'd be surprised what you can learn about a person if you take the time to look beneath the surface, right, Driskoll?"

"Right." Driskoll fingered the seeing gem one last time and slipped it back in his pocket. "It's just a matter of seeing things clearly."

"True Knights of the Silver Dragon can always see clearly," Zendric said. The wizard smiled warmly at Driskoll, Kellach, and Moyra.

"Now," Zendric said, slapping his hands on the table. "Didn't someone say something about dessert?"

Enter a World of Adventure

Do you want to learn more about the world of Krynn?
Look for these and other DRAGONLANCE® books in the fantasy section
of your local bookstore or library.

Titles by Margaret Weis and Tracy Hickman

Legends Trilogy

Time of the Twins, War of the Twins, and Test of the Twins

A wizard weaves a plan to conquer darkness—
and bring it under his control.

The Second Generation

The sword passes to a new generation of heroes—
the children of the Heroes of the Lance.

Dragons of Summer Flame

A young mage seeks to enter the Abyss in search of his lost uncle,
the infamous Raistlin.

The War of Souls Trilogy

Dragons of a Fallen Star, Dragons of a Lost Star, Dragons of a Vanished Moon

A new war begins, one more terrible than any in Krynn have ever known.

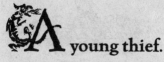 young thief.
A wizard's apprentice.
A twelve-year-old boy.
Meet the Knights of
the Silver Dragon!

Secret of the Spiritkeeper
Matt Forbeck

Can Moyra, Kellach, and Driskoll unlock the secret of the
spiritkeeper in time to rescue their beloved wizard friend?

August 2004

Riddle in Stone
Ree Soesbee

Will the Knights unravel the statue's riddle
before more people turn to stone?

August 2004

Sign of the Shapeshifter
Dale Donovan and Linda Johns

Can Kellach and Driskoll find the shapeshifter
before he ruins their father?

October 2004

Eye of Fortune
Denise R. Graham

Does the fortuneteller's prophecy spell doom
for the Knights? Or unheard-of treasure?

December 2004

For ages 8 and up

THE NEW ADVENTURES

JOIN A GROUP OF FRIENDS AS THEY UNLOCK MYSTERIES OF THE **DRAGONLANCE®** WORLD!

TEMPLE OF THE DRAGONSLAYER
Tim Waggoner

Nearra has lost all memory of who she is. With newfound friends, she ventures to an ancient temple where she may uncover her past. Visions of magic haunt her thoughts. And someone is watching.

July 2004

THE DYING KINGDOM
Stephen D. Sullivan

In a near-forgotten kingdom, an ancient evil lurks. As Nearra's dark visions grow stronger, her friends must fight for their lives.

July 2004

THE DRAGON WELL
Dan Willis

Battling a group of bandits, the heroes unleash the mystic power of a dragon well. And none of them will ever be the same.

September 2004

RETURN OF THE SORCERESS
Tim Waggoner

When Nearra and her friends confront the wizard who stole her memory, their faith in each other is put to the ultimate test.

November 2004

For ages 10 and up

WANT TO KNOW HOW IT ALL BEGAN?

WANT TO KNOW MORE ABOUT THE DRAGONLANCE® WORLD?

FIND OUT IN THIS NEW BOXED SET OF THE FIRST DRAGONLANCE TITLES!

A RUMOR OF DRAGONS
Volume 1

NIGHT OF THE DRAGONS
Volume 2

THE NIGHTMARE LANDS
Volume 3

TO THE GATES OF PALANTHAS
Volume 4

HOPE'S FLAME
Volume 5

A DAWN OF DRAGONS
Volume 6

Gift Set available September 2004
By Margaret Weis & Tracy Hickman
For ages 10 and up